✸GOLD LUST✸

by

CHARLES NUETZEL

WRITING AS "ALBERT AUGUSTUS, JR."

The Borgo Press
An Imprint of Wildside Press

MMVII

To my **Brother**,
who needs always to be reminded
that life is a one-time event.
Make the most of it.

SECOND EDITION

❋CONTENTS❋

✹INTRODUCTION✹

This is one of those adventure stories that have always fascinated me. The first one I wrote was *Lost City of the Damned* and I wrote a number of others, some of which are coming out in Wildside editions. They all were influenced and inspired by my early love of the Edgar Rice Burroughs novels.

I have always been fascinated by lost civilizations and have managed to actually visit some ruins in Mesoamerica, seeing the Mayan, Aztec, and Inca sites on our side of the world, and recently the pyramids of Egypt. It can be an amazing experience to walk among these ancient structures and imagine what kind of people might have lived there. The memory of their existence is fairly well lost in time, yet one can let their minds imagine all kinds of fanciful visions of a people long gone.

Touching the stones, walking the pathways, or even up the magnificent pyramids themselves, is breathtaking, and inspiring in ways that stay with you for a very long time. And you begin to wonder...

Gold Lust is the story about three people who get involved in a nasty triangle of lust and greed, and a search for ancient treasure on an island in the South Pacific where the remains of an ancient civilization protects a mysterious temple and its idol of gold.

Steve Floyd, the hero of *Gold Lust*, is a somewhat lost soul, barely surviving day to day by chartering his small seaplane to anyone needing a joy ride. When Virginia Donovan came into his life, offering a couple thousand dollars to take her to a distant island that very night, he was instantly intrigued. Not since the death of his wife, years before, had he found any female so visually exciting. Most men would sell their souls to take her into their arms.

But Virginia comes with a nasty partner, who must be her lover. Yet she makes no attempt to hide her interest in Steve. She could be had for the taking. Or was she playing him for a fool? He could never tell if she was a Goddess of Love or a demon from hell. And there was no question that the woman was dangerous, willing to do anything to get what she wanted!

Yet he fell totally under her spell and rediscovered feelings he had thought long dead.

Virginia Donovan leads him to a golden Virgin Idol locked away in the ancient temple ruins of a lost civilization. A curse was supposed to have protected it for at least a thousand years.

Now, tell me, what could be more normal? Love, passion, betrayal, violence, an ancient ruin and a mysterious curse all packed up in the promise of riches beyond a normal person's wildest nightmare.

Well, that's the kind of stuff that dreams are made of, as they say in cornball movies and novels. And one can almost believe such things could happen after you have touched an ancient stone, climbed up the side of an ancient pyramid and looked across the expanse of ruins left for hundreds and thousands of years for anyone to marvel at.

I'm a romantic, I suppose. And I will never stop being fascinated by such places, such visions, such stories of adventure in distant places.

—CHARLES NUETZEL
Thousand Oaks, California
July 2006

❋ONE❋

As usual, Steve Floyd was drunk. He was lounging in the Sea Cove, a small saloon just opposite the dock at Shell Island.

The rum had tasted good in the beginning, but now it was too sweet. His throat was beginning to burn from too much of the stuff; his vision blurred. He sat there at the small wooden table holding his head in his hands thinking about the mess his last little trip had turned into.

The place was dimly lighted and what little light came from outside cast only sharp outlines on his ruggedly handsome face. When the tall woman came up to his table and asked, "Are you Steven Floyd?" it took several seconds for him to react.

He had been thinking about the long trip he had taken with Mary-Lou, his small seaplane, in search of a yacht that had given an SOS signal the night before. What he discovered wasn't worth having gone out for. The yacht had crashed into a reef and the three passengers had disappeared into the depths of the Pacific Ocean.

"Are you Mr. Floyd?" the woman's voice persisted.

Steve blinked and shook his head to clear away the fog. Slowly he turned his gray-blue eyes in the direction of the voice. What met his gaze was startling enough to knock the drunken blur from his mind in one shocking jolt.

The woman was tall, high-breasted, and curvy. She was decked out in a form-fitting light skirt and white blouse which did plenty for her figure. Her, face, with high cheekbones and wide lips, gave a classic and sensual appearance that attracted his immediate attention.

Her long blonde hair flowed over her shoulders in lush waves, framing her face in a most attractive way.

She didn't look like one of the rich women of the islands, or one of the tourists or natives. The expression in her deep blue eyes was striking, probing, as if she were desperate. She seemed to ignore the obvious sweep of his eyes, rushing all over her.

"I'm Floyd, yes. What can I do for you?" he said, slurring the words. He stumbled to his feet in an awkward attempt to be gentlemanly.

She sighed out her relief and then fell into the chair opposite his.

"Oh, God, I'm glad to find you at last! I wasn't sure. You look different from what Hal Jenkins described you."

Steve steadied himself by gripping hold of the table and then slowly allowed himself to fall onto his chair again.

"What can I do for you? I take it you know Hal?"

"He recommended you," she told him. "I'm in desperate need of help, and he said you would be willing to help me."

Steve studied her, and the more he looked the

more pleased he was. Some time back he had helped
Hal Jenkins out of a jam with the local authorities.
Hal was one of those playboy types who had played
once too often and with the wrong women. It had
happened some years back.

"How is Hal?" Steve inquired.

"Married, since last year." She paused. "We
grew up together. He said you would help me—for
a price."

Her lips smiled on that last word, as if subtly
suggesting more than money. But the woman made
no point of pushing that in his face—as much as he
would have loved her to do so.

Steve grinned to himself and thought that the
price wouldn't be too high at all, if he ever got a
chance to explore her magnificent figure. It had
been some time since he'd had a white woman.
Dreamland, that. Why would a classy lady like this
want to climb into bed with a drunken bum like
him? But every man had the right to dream.

"What can I do for you, then? What's the prob-
lem?"

"Well, I don't have much time—we'll have to
start right away. But it'll be worth expenses and two
thousand dollars if you'll help me." Her voice was
brisk and businesslike. But her eyes met his in a
rather frank probing. For what he wasn't sure. Yet
there seemed to be just a twinkling fume of smoke
hidden in her gaze. And with smoke came fire. And
with fire, from this lady, could come one hell of a
blast of overwhelming heat.

He forced the thought out of his mind.

You're dreaming, he told himself. Of course, it
costs nothing to dream.

Steve nodded. "You'll have to say that again. I'm a little under the bottle right now." He pointed to the bottle of rum on the table. "You *did* say two thousand?"

She nodded. "I'll come right to the point, Mr. Floyd. I don't like beating around the bush, so to speak. And with a man like you I believe it is smart to just lay it out on the table and see if you … see if you pick it up and—" She broke off, as if having said something totally different than her mere words implied. And even taken on face value they somehow contained a subtle double meaning. "Now, don't get the wrong idea. I wouldn't want you to do that, Mr. Floyd."

"Steve," he smiled. For some reason he felt she wanted him to get the wrong meaning.

"Steve. Okay, Steve." She seemed to caress over his name, part thoughtfully, part caressingly. Her eyes continued to gaze evenly into his. And her voice was once again all business. "Now, my brother is some sort of a fortune hunter—he has more money than he ever needs. But he's after art treasures from lost civilizations.

"He disappeared two months ago, and the only evidence I have is a letter from him. I'm scared to death!" She opened her purse and took out a letter, which she handed to him. Accidentally her fingers touched his, lingering just slightly on contact. Then they almost jerked away when he took the offered paper.

For a moment he simply watched her, aware of that fiery tingle which had surged through him, as if her fingers had been charged. He couldn't help letting his eyes sweep once again over her voluptuous body, lingering almost hungrily over its fine, firm curves.

The woman sat there, unmoving, assessing him as equally intense with her eyes. Neither said a thing, but his mind was racing with all kinds of opening lines to invite a swift flirtation right into her arms.

Was it imagination or was she literally egging him on? Did she want him to flirt? Did she want to be grabbed and tossed onto the floor and ravished?

If they were in his plane or anywhere alone, he would have found it very difficult to ignore the implication of that momentary connection. Real or imagined.

Nervously he looked away, then spread the letter on the table and peered at the handwriting. It took some doing to make out the words because his vision was in pretty sad shape by now.

He skimmed over the first lines, which were personal and seemed of no interest. It was when he came to the mention of the Akiki Virgin Idol that his brain was jolted. He had heard stories about a Virgin Idol, cast in gold, which was supposed to have been the symbol of love for a primitive civilization that had existed on a small island some three hundred miles from where they were now. It was legend, and Steve had never been one to believe the stories that islanders told.

The Idol was supposed to have been cursed— the whole island cursed. And the civilization had disappeared, people and all, leaving only the ruins which existed now in the depths of the jungle. Several people had gone after the Idol but had never found it. Instead they had found strange and mysterious deaths. Nobody had searched for the last couple of hundred years though, so all of it was merely superstition from his point of view.

The letter read:

> *...I've finally gotten a real lead on the Akiki Virgin Idol, Virginia. I can't tell you much about it in a letter because there are others who have become interested, too. This much I can tell you. It's supposed to be in a buried temple, under the ruins of the Akiki City, on Akiki Island.*
>
> *I'm sure, this time. I followed through on the evidence I discovered in the States, and I've come up with the first evidence of the temple in my diggings. I'm returning to Akiki tomorrow. I had to get supplies for a month's stay. You'll hear from me in four weeks and—*

Steve looked up at the woman. "So? He said you would hear from him..."

"That was other two months ago! He never—*never*—has gone back on his word. I'm frightened. I have to go out to Akiki and find out what happened to him. I'm afraid that...something terrible has happened!" Her voice was choked and husky. There was just the suggestion of tears welling in her eyes.

"But surely he could have been detained and—"

"No. That's final! Will you help me get out there?" she announced.

Steve was thoughtful for a moment, then sighed. "For two thousand dollars I'd do anything."

14

"Can we leave right away?"

"Well, Miss—"

"Virginia Donovan."

"Miss Donovan. Not before this evening. It's impossible," he told her, thinking about his lightly boozed up state. It would take that much time for me to completely sober up enough to fly.

Virginia Donovan hesitated and then finally nodded.

"Okay, meet me at the Harmon Hotel at six." With that she stood and quickly left the saloon.

GOLD LUST, BY CHARLES NUETZEL

❋TWO❋

Virginia was smiling triumphantly to herself as she stepped into the hotel room which she'd taken with Ed Blondall. Ed, a large thick shouldered man with almost beautifully handsome features, leaped from the bed. He rushed to her, grabbing hold of her shoulders and crushing her body tightly against his.

"Well?" His voice was harsh.

"He fell, Hook, line, and...sucker...well, sinker."

Ed Blondall gave out with a low, animal grunt, then kissed her roughly.

As the kiss broke away, Virginia felt the building need drive through her, felt the wild, hungry madness cut at every muscle and nerve. The look in his eyes brought a throaty laugh from her lips. Ed was a hard, muscular man who knew how to please a girl—how to make her go wild with need.

And Virginia was, strongly sexed and had enjoyed being with a man since she was in her late teens. Long before that she'd found it impossible not to have many sexual fantasies.

Ed was a special kind of male animal and she especially appreciated his powerhouse body. They were good together.

They had known each other for some time now.

17

A little less than the time she'd been divorced from her ex-husband, Ralph Donovan.

Anger and bitterness choked at Virginia at the thought of how Ralph Donovan had left her without a penny. It was his own fault that she'd been sleeping out on him. His body just didn't give her all she needed. He could have been a little more understanding. But things were about to be turned around. He wouldn't have the law on his side, now; not out there on Akiki Island.

And even more important, the Virgin Idol would be much better in her hands than in Ralph's. He would turn it over to the authorities—to some damned dusty museum—and a lot of good it would do anybody!

Virginia stretched out on the bed and reached for Ed, whose hard, heavy shoulders were so powerful and lovely to touch. She hardly loved the man, but enjoyed his body to the fullest. The touch of those large hands had always sent voluptuous waves through her. It was like being taken by a gorilla; a wild, exciting gorilla. Almost brutally driven to a rapid peak of energetic pleasure.

As he joined her, she tensed against him, scraping her long, tapered fingernails against the rigid muscles of his back. She went fiery all over, burning with greedy need for what he was so good at giving her.

"Oh, Ed, just go for it!" she moaned, pressing up against him, suddenly dizzy in the grip of his large strong body. Her hands were all over him, anxiously stripping him naked while his caresses were equally greedy in removing her clothing. There was no pre-amble to their love-making. It was

18

savage and demanding and fully charged the instant their naked flesh made contact.

That was the way Ed drove her; beyond any limits, right into the heavy embrace of total ecstasy.

* * * * * * *

Steve Floyd stepped into the shower, turned on the icy water, and wanted to scream against the shivering coldness that attacked his naked body.

"Hell!" he cursed, shaking his head, trying to blast away the buzzing effect of the booze. "Hell...*Hell!*"

Finally he stepped out of the shower and dried himself. Looking into the small bedroom, he remembered the native, half-caste woman who had been in there the other night, drunk and passionate as all hell. She'd been a hellion. Damned good.

Shaking himself, Steve moved to the mirror and looked at his ruddy features, at the square angle of his jaw, the curve of his lips and nose. It was a good, strong face—but not really handsome. The nose was a little large, though not protruding. His flesh was darkly tanned from long days in the sun.

"You have a hell of a life," he told his fate. "A real bum!"

Yet that wasn't quite true. In the beginning there had been a real purpose in life. But in the last years, since the death of his wife, Janice, Steve had simply sunk into a pattern that had no direction other than living from day to day. Finding his kicks when they came, making a little money jockeying rich people around the islands in his sea plane or going out on a rescue mission when necessary. Ends met—one way or another.

Life had started out fairly well for Steve, and when he had married Janice Decker, everything had seemed beautiful and wonderful. They were an ideal couple in every way. He worshipped her from head to foot. Her very soul had interlocked with his so totally that nothing much touched him after her death.

He'd been a pilot in the Air Force a few years before, and between the two of them they had gotten up enough money to buy a plane. During their marriage, Steve had managed a fairly good living.

Then, when Janice was killed in an auto accident one night, seven years before, Steve had gone out on a drunken binge which had continued for well over six months. Then he traded in his plane for the sea-job he now owned. He came out to the islands to settle, away from the old memories and old friends he had known with Janice. Since then he had drifted. And the only female pleasures came from native girls. They were a pleasant distraction, a sexual release when he was in a half-drunken state.

But none of them could fill the empty space which Janice's death had created. Since then everything had gone to dust inside his soul, leaving nothing but an empty shell. He'd survived by simply stumbling through each day, a bottle in one hand and, when needed, a native girl with whom to spend the night hours.

Maybe it was time to change things, he told himself. That was a mantra that haunted every morning hangover.

How long could he continue dancing around the empty shell he'd become?

Well, the two thousand this broad, Virginia Donovan, was offering certainly could be a starter.

"Bull," he growled. Yet if he could just care enough to leap past the empty void in his life, maybe things could be different.

As Steve fixed himself some coffee, his mind pictured his new client, and a vague knife of interest moved through him. She was one hell of a broad. There had been something about her, regardless of the all-business attitude, which had suggested a real woman— the kind who was ready and willing to go the full bedroom route. The idea intrigued him. Though that was probably nothing but a pipe-dream.

Still, any man would jump through hoops to have her in his arms.

After coffee, Steve went down into the lobby and was suddenly brought up short by one hefty, short, dark-haired female. She wore a low-cut printed blouse, which gave an excellent view of her frontal development.

The little hot firecracker from the other night. Linni.

"Hi, Steve. When you get back?" she asked, flirting with her large brown eyes. "I heard you were back—came to see how things were."

What a brazen woman this is, he thought, both annoyed and intrigued. He couldn't really remember too much detail about the other evening.

Steve looked at the clock above the hotel desk and then back at Linni who stood before him. He had no doubt about what she was offering. It might be some days before he got a tumble—unless something developed between this Virginia Donovan and himself, and that was highly uncertain.

In fact he wrote that off as nonsense.

He had known Linni for a long time, off and on, but not until the other night had they tumbled into the rack together. She worked at one of the hangouts he enjoyed. He'd been good and high the other night, and good and ready for any willing woman. She had flirted as usual, and he'd decided to make a direct pass to Go.

Now her eyes were flirting in the same way— large, dark, smoldering eyes, which promised as much as they were pleading for.

It was four in the afternoon.

"I don't have much time right now," he told her. "Have to leave by six." But his hand was already holding onto her soft arm. "Yet...if you don't mind keeping me company for that long..."

She snickered and pressed her hip against his in a most inviting way. They turned and left the lobby together.

❋ THREE ❋

Steve was just checking through the controls when Virginia entered the small cockpit and sat in the co-pilot's seat. She eyed him in a strangely pleasant way, her face almost smiling.

"I hope you don't mind that I forgot to mention Ed," she said.

"Why should I?" he countered.

It had been a surprise to find that there was another person going on the trip with them. He had pictured a pleasant little relationship between himself and "Ginny"—as Ed called her. Maybe it wouldn't make any difference anyway.

When he'd picked them up at their hotel, they were in the cocktail lounge where all three had a round of drinks on Ginny.

Now, with her so close to him, more or less "alone," Steve leaned back and smiled at her, letting his eyes run down her figure. Her legs were extremely inviting. It was going to be hard to spend time with this woman without any chance at all for a little serious flirtation. At least a little, harmless flirtation between two healthy animals didn't hurt anybody. So he grinned rather wolfishly at her.

"Think I'm pretty?" she asked warmly.

What a change from this afternoon, Steve

thought. Maybe it was the drinks.

"You're very pretty—if that's the word for it. I could think of some more...well, how would I say it?"

"How would I know? She laughed throatily, just letting him gaze at her, enjoying it without comment.

"Well, if pretty is enough to satisfy you. It was your word, not mine."

"And what might your words be?" she inquired, all innocence.

"Well, all things considered, you're one hell of a...well...pretty lady." He let his eyes linger at her breasts and hips, then slide back up to her face. She was smiled, amused.

"Just a pretty lady, now that's interesting. Considering what you're eyes just did to me."

"Now, what was that?"

"I'm not going to tell. I'm a lady. And lady's don't say such things to a strange man."

"I'm that strange?"

"Well...let's say we don't know one another that well."

"Hopefully that'll chance in the next days."

"I bet you sure would like that," she almost giggled in delight. It was a low, rich giggle, not a girlish one and a hot electric caress raced down his spine. "But, I suppose I have to be a nice, pretty lady at her best."

"Is that the best you can do?"

"Hardly. But...I'm not telling." She laughed at that in a very playful way. "You're fun! Maybe we'll have fun teasing one another...that is innocent enough, even for a pretty lady. Respectable. You know."

"Yeah. Sure. Gotta be respectable and all that."

"Would you mind terribly if I sat up here with you? I've never been in the cockpit of a plane before. It sounds exciting."

"Make yourself at home—but won't your boyfriend mind?"

"Ed? Oh, don't be silly. We're just friends. Buddies. I needed somebody to—well, escort me—that's all. Didn't want to go out in the world all alone." She laughed. "I need my gorilla man to muscle the dangers away. And…then, too, I do need a man of a gorilla to…watch over me. Well." She shrugged. "I'm a pretty lady. I think that'll have to define the moment."

For some reason he couldn't help believing that she was lying about Ed. That man looked like a muscular gorilla type who wouldn't just stand around and look without touching. He pushed that thought out of his mind.

"Well, we might as well get started." That could have two meanings, but quite obviously it didn't. He'd just love to get started on something very intimate with this hot package.

God, I'm hoary! He mentally groaned. And who wouldn't be with this dish just within reach. He could smell her perfume like a drug seducing his normal male hormones.

It was difficult to believe she wasn't aware, exactly, how effective her nearness was. The woman might be just playing for fun; on the other hand there could be some other motive in her mind.

Oh, if it only matched his own ever-building desires.

"How long will it take?" she asked.

Had she read his mind?

He reconsidered, then realized what she'd asked about: "We should land by night fall. I just don't see what all the hurry is about."

Her frown stopped him. "I didn't want to delay for a moment."

Somehow Steve felt as if that involved far more than she was offering. No matter what, the woman appeared on the surface one thing and under all that gloss and refined outer layer, and the rather sophisticatedly amused flirtatious manner, there was something engagingly unsettling about her. The contrasts were confusing and somewhat very seductive.

Instinct warned me that the trip was going to be one wild ride, either through Pleasureland or Hell City. Maybe both.

* * * * * * *

As Virginia looked at the man, she felt a strange animal attraction toward him. A normal heat generated from him to her. A body-alert automatically sparked by his animal appeal. In the bar he had looked different—a little crusty, dirty and seedy. Now, seeing him sober and completely in control of himself, and in his surroundings, in his own plane, the appeal of the man was sharp and bold. Starkly so. She literally felt a flush tremble through her at the thought of what could so very easily take place between the two of them.

She sighed, thinking how impossible it would be to allow any intimacy to develop. Her life was de-

voted to Ed Blondall—at least until she'd gotten
what she wanted.

The thought intrigued her. Here was a man,
Steve Floyd, an adventurer who had knocked
around for a long time. From what she'd learned
about the man he was ripe to be picked up by some
sharp girl and snapped back to full bloom—away
from bumming around the world. She enjoyed playing with the exciting idea. But then, Virginia told
herself, she played with such ideas about any man
she came across. Men did things to her—making her
wild. She had been like than since her teens. When a
male looked at her body she almost swooned as a
kid starting to develop breasts.

She watched as Steve Floyd went through the
final checks. She watched his intense, alert and intelligent eyes and his large strong hands. He wasn't
as broad as Ed, but looked as strong, in a different
way. Ed was brutal—a savage. Virginia couldn't
help thinking that Steve was something different,
cut from another block. Maybe quite skilled as a
lover. At least well worth the sampling.

"Okay," Steve announced, turning to look at
her. "Strap in. We're off in a minute."

"Rockets alive?" she laughed. "Sputtering all
over the place?" And her own mind was imagining
all kinds of images, which those words might actually be describing. A flush of hot desire raced
through her once again as she watched the man.

"Alive and firing!" he told her, body quite tense
so she could see the muscles tighten visibly.

Oh to have those in her hands, to have him taking her in those wonderfully powerful looking arms.
To feast on this male beast!

She shook her head almost savagely, attempting to block such thoughts. Silly little teasing and flirtation was one thing, but letting things go beyond that with the "hired" help was simply foolish.

And her body was just pleased to be wildly foolish and to hell with the rules.

* * * * * * *

Ed Blondall sat in the passenger compartment brooding. He didn't like the set-up. He didn't mind that Virginia was going to play it cool with this Floyd guy. He just didn't like letting her get that close to another man, at least while he was around to feed on the lushness of that body of hers.

Of all the women Ed Blondall had known in his life—and there had been many—Ginny Donovan took top honors. He'd never known a woman who could come on like Ginny.

Man, from the first time he'd seen her at the bar that night, all bagged out to give hell to any man willing to take up the challenge, he'd been hooked for sure. Sex at first sight.

Then the bed routine. He hadn't expected anything like it. She had asked for everything he could give her, as if this were the first time for her in ages and she'd held back for much too long. At first Ed had believed she'd been just hard up. Later he learned that it got better—that she couldn't get enough.

As time went on he learned more and more about Ginny Donovan and her cold, older husband who had more money than he knew what to do with. Ralph Donovan was a bug on ancient treasures, civilizations, cities, and cultures. It was the old man's hobby. When his wife should have been his full time occupation.

It had been Ed's idea to sneak in on the next take; see to it that there was some sort of accident which would leave ex-hubby lost and dead in one of his old, ancient, lost cities. To hell with giving gold and treasures to City Hall. Just one treasure would set him up good. And with Ginny around for a while, until he got tired of her demanding hunger, it would be kicks, all over the world. Ginny was one great kick girl. Not for keeps, but for kicks. Then kick her out.

Ed had given a lot of thought to what he would do with the money once it got into his hot sweaty hands. Life had been real crap for him: born poor, on the poor side of the city; father who drank too much and banged anything with skirts on; mother who was nothing better than a whore. His childhood had taught him to grab what he could get and run like hell.

The world owed him something. And with Ginny for kicks, he would get a good piece of what it owed him. He would dump Ginny when the time came. A man couldn't trust a woman like her for long. Her physical needs were overpowering—but fun, as long as his own nerves could stand it.

Yet, sitting there as the engines of the sea plane warmed up, Ed felt anger cutting through him at the thought of Virginia playing up to the flyer. He didn't like Steve Floyd, and it was going to be a pleasure to cut him down to size when the time came.

The plane started moving and Ed felt himself

pressed slightly back against the seat.

Maybe Ginny knew what she was doing, he thought. This Stevie boy could become a hard cat if times got difficult. Hell, he really wouldn't mind the girl giving out a little to the guy—just to keep him in line a bit. Heck there was one hell of a lot of her to go around and no one man seemed able to fully satisfy her greedy body.

They would have to get off the island, leave Akiki, once they'd gotten the loot.

The plane soared into the sky, tipped slightly, banked, and then slowly swooped upwards.

Ed looked out the window and shuddered. He hated flying and he hated the sea. He'd never learned how to swim and the seemingly endless expanse of the ocean always gave him a fright. Flying was another kind of terror. If anything happened to the plane, there was only one way to go—down, to death.

He shuddered again and then turned away. He looked at the closed door of the cockpit and seethed silently.

Hell, he thought, what difference did it make what Ginny thought or did, just so he got controlling interest in the money? And anyway, he controlled Ginny. When she'd suggested that they play it cool and act like just friends, let Floyd think he had a chance to cut into something real hot, Ed had played the part of the hurt lover. Yet he knew it really couldn't make that much difference.

He patted the gun that was tucked away in his shoulder holster. If things went sour, there were always those little charming bullets waiting to even things out—to balance them his way, regardless.

❋FOUR❋

The flight was long and uneventful for Steve Floyd, outside of the obvious pleasure of being next to such a woman as Virginia Donovan. Her dark slacks and tight mannish shirt did nothing to hide her figure. In fact the way she was dressed accented every lovely curve.

They talked about the workings of the plane and she questioned him about his past life. She sounded quite intrigued when he mentioned that he'd been bumming around for some time. It was as if the idea seemed almost exciting to her.

"A lot of girls?" she asked.

"Some," he admitted, then added, "But I'd rather think of them as woman. Not into children, mind you."

She merely smiled at that, knowingly, then teasingly said: "Sometimes…one forgets how it was back then. So many hormones pumping. Not saying they are like a gushing well…well, still, that is. A girl…well, lady just gets better, don't you think?"

"Well, maturity brings along some very nice benefits," he chuckled.

"I bet there are many willing…ladies just fluttering all around your…well…net."

"What makes you say that?" His eyes snapped

31

once again to her figure.

"You look like the kind a full blown, mature male that a woman would find hot, that's all."

"Why, I think you're flirting with me."

"Apparently not at all. I mean, when I flirt with a man he *knows* it, no thinking about it, honey."

"Just my damn luck," he offered lightly, trying hard to ignore the throaty sound of her voice.

"Well, don't be so disappointed. I'm sure you have your pick. Why, you're the very image of the typical adventurer who is so popular on television."

"This isn't TV, lady."

"Well, if it were, you'd be the star of some adventure show. Out there in the islands where ladies in trouble would come your way, seeking help and then love in your arms. A lot of girls—in the stories, of course—would be broken heartedly left behind. Can't have the star getting involved into some romantic tangle with a lady, death to an on-going series."

"But this isn't a television show, now is it?"

"I suspect not, How disappointing!"

"And I ain't no damn actor playing some dumb stud part."

"Why, Steve, you sound rather annoyed by that."

"Well, if I were one of those guys you'd be in my arms right now!" he laughed in delight, feeling he'd check-mated her.

Not missing a beat she said: "Do you want to be one of...oh!" She broke off, laughed throatily. "My, you had me fooled! Almost had me there!"

And of course she wasn't fooled at all. She had dropped right into his word-trap, danced around it and counter-mated him in one little retort.

He didn't know exactly what to say at that point, and she didn't help him at all.

The atmosphere seemed to have elevated several degrees hotter between them. Going much further might be entering a rather tropic zone neither of them was about to dive into at the moment—if ever.

The conversation dwindled after that.

Just before they sighted the island of Akiki, Steve asked again, "Why are you so all fired up to get going, so fast? I mean, this very evening. We won't be able to do anything until tomorrow. And it won't be very comfortable, sleeping in the plane tonight."

Virginia laughed in delight at that.

"What's so funny?"

"Oh, best I don't tell. If you knew what's going on inside my mind..." She shrugged, as if it didn't matter, almost as if she wanted him to beg her to tell him. But her next words smothered over the implied suggestion. "I'm worried—and I couldn't wait. I've always been like that. I wanted to get on the ball...Oh, God, I said a no-no!"

She really laughed at that, very low and throatily. "Oh, I'm in big trouble now!"

She hesitated at that line, then continued, a gleam in her eyes. "I don't want to waste a minute. That's better. I hate to give the wrong impression."

"Why do I find that difficult to believe."

"What?"

"You giving the wrong impression. I think you're quite clever!"

She simply smiled, then offered: "Once I make up my mind about something, I move. And fast! I supposed that's clear enough, right?"

She threw her head back, giving him a wonderful view of her creamy smooth throat and neck. Her breasts bulged against the blouse.

Then he spotted a small dot on the far horizon. Pointing, Steve said: "Well, there it is!"

* * * * * * *

They had settled down in a small cove. Akiki Island was a volcanic peak in the middle of the Pacific Ocean, shaped in the curving arch of a small C. A natural cove gave a perfect place to set up evening camp. Once the plane had been secured, Steve went into the passenger compartment and started folding chairs back, forming them into three beds.

"Not much like home, but it'll have to do. Since you're in such a hurry."

Night had settled. The ocean around them, inside the cove, was calm and quiet. Only the sound of tropic insects and night birds, with the occasional moan of a wild beast, sounded from the land a few yards away.

Steve opened a back compartment, revealing a small cooking stove and a pantry, which held a supply of food.

"Anybody for a drink?" he offered, opening another small compartment.

Both Ed and Virginia yelped, "All the comforts of home!

Virginia cried, "I could really use something like that!"

Steve poured drinks. Three dark, heavy-bodied rums.

34

"Here's to you," he said, after handing the drinks over.

He found it hard to keep his eyes away from Virginia. What a woman, he thought.

That long blonde hair, deep blue flashing flirting eyes that seemed to promise so damned much. She never missed a beat in connecting with him, letting wordless glances embrace him like loving, electric arms.

It might have been his imagination, but he suspected not. She enjoyed letting him just feast on her body. It was as if she had presented herself on stage and expected to be fairly devoured by the audience—in this case—one. Ed didn't seem to count. The man was background "noise"!

That lush figure just stretched out no matter in what position, sitting formally or relaxed. It was a continual display of sexuality. Her muscle tone was lovely, and every movement she made just kept accenting the amazing perfection of her body.

Then he remembered the story she had told him in the afternoon. That didn't fit with her blatant flirtatious attitude. She didn't look like the type of woman who was worried about a lost brother. She was more like a hell-cat on the make—celebrating and excited at the idea of being there with two men, one who was probably her lover and another who wanted to be.

But then, women like Virginia had to be used to having men stare as if she were a delicious all night meal.

Something stabbed at the back of his mind like a warning bell. There was definitely something wrong about the whole setup.

Then he gulped on the rum and let it burn down his throat as he tossed aside the thoughts.

So maybe she was just a kook. So maybe she was happy to be on the way. So maybe she was a spoiled little rich bitch.

Maybe the woman just got off being ogled by men. Many a woman he'd known was like that. They enjoyed the flirtatious game as a beginning and end all unto itself. They were teases and enjoyed teasing more than having sex with a man.

Maybe that was Virginia's game.

What difference did it make to him? She was paying expenses and two thousand dollars besides.

Steve glanced at Ed Blondall. There was a hard customer. The kind of guy women went for, but who played it for kicks. He had met men like Ed before—and he didn't like them. Brutal, uncaring SOBs who simply rammed a woman without much sensitivity for her feelings.

Sure, Steve told himself, *he played girls for kicks and used women when they were using him.*

But this Ed guy would use a woman to get his own thrills—and whatever else he wanted—and then split the scene. Bash and run.

That was the basic difference.

Beyond that, Steve hadn't missed the slight bulge of the gun and shoulder holster. Not that they didn't have a right to be armed against any trouble, but he couldn't help thinking that this was the kind of man who carried a gun around most of his waking hours, and no doubt slept with it under his pillow at night.

Instinctively he didn't like the man.

"Well," Steve said, smiling, "what say we consider organizing a dinner?"

Virginia shook her head. "Nothing doin'. I'll treat—if you'll take a rain check. I much prefer having a party."

Her eyes flashed to Ed. The interchange was startling. The air seemed to crackle with emotion.

Ed said: "You know what booze does to you, hon."

"Slam it down and button it up, Ed! I want to booze it!" she cried, a gleam in her eyes.

"Help yourself," Steve offered, pouring another shot for himself. He wondered just what alcohol did to this woman. Was it a turn on? Would she end up stripping and taking both of them on in an orgy meant for three?

He'd known women like that. But the idea of sharing her with an animal like Ed—even the idea of her being with that man—was not at all a nice one.

Steve just hoped nothing took place he couldn't keep under control.

* * * * * * *

An hour had passed, and Virginia was feeling drunk and nervous. It had been a mistake to drink, she told herself, sitting in one of the seats that hadn't been folded down for a bed.

The men were fixing quick hamburgers. As she watched them, her mind revolved with the erotic record that always sang over and over when she was in the presence of men.

The drinks had dissolved all the resistance, which she'd felt earlier.

Virginia jerked to her feet and moved to join the men.

"Mind if I have another snort?" she asked, pressing against Steve's side. She noticed how the man tensed. She reached for the bottle.

Pouring herself a stiff drink, she let her hip once more "accidentally" brush the flyer's. He felt solidly muscled, like hard steel.

Ed said: "Cut the drinking, Ginny."

"Lay off, Ed! You don't own me!" she snapped. Her eyes flared as ripping seething rage burst through her.

Damn Ed! Damn men! They think they own you.

But the more sober portion of Virginia's mind said, *No, you are tied to Ed, and you can't cross him too far.*

To hell with that, she screamed silently, tipping the glass and gulping.

Suddenly a hard hand gripped her arm brutally and jerked at her.

"Come here!" Ed growled, half shoving her toward the cockpit. "I'd better talk to you."

He glanced at Steve. "Sorry, old man but...you understand."

Furious, Virginia let Ed shove her into the pilot's compartment. He closed the door behind him, glaring at her. "What's the idea?"

"I...I can't stand this!" she moaned, suddenly and vividly aware that they were alone. Her drunken mind saw the opportunity this offered. She didn't consider how impossible it might be. She reached for Ed, even while not really wanting him, but hot to get intimate with Steve. That conversation earlier with the pilot had carved fiery brands of desire in her brain.

But Ed was better than nothing. And she was drunk enough not to care.

"Cut that out!" he cursed in a husky voice. "Cool off!"

Virginia laughed. "Come on, Eddy. Be good!"

She thrust herself against him.

"You bitch, you'll kill everything!" he snarled.

"The hell I will!" she moaned. "I can't stand it, Ed. You know how I am when I have booze. And this...I'm swimming...honestly, Ed. God, help me!"

Every nerve was burning as if red-hot fires had flicked them. Her whole body seethed with raging need. She knew the feeling; she knew what it was going to do to her.

"I told you to cut the drinks!" he snapped. Then he shoved her away forcefully. "You stay here, until you've cool off!"

He turned to leave.

Virginia was wild now, unable to control the hot desire bubbling over her.

She threw her arms around his neck, drawing her body against him. "Please, Ed. You know I can't stand it. You know how I am. Please!"

Brutally, as if he almost enjoyed it, Ed twisted and shoved her back. Then his right hand slashed out, striking her face and jarring her head to one side.

"Cool down! There's too much at stake," he warned.

Dazed, Virginia sobbed against the pain of the blow, and watched Ed leave.

For a long time she stood there, trying hard to control the emotion—the tense, grinding, overwhelming desire—which was now in complete control of her. It was hell to be trapped in this body of hers. It controlled everything she did, every thought she had, every action and reaction. It had ruined her marriage to Ralph Donovan. But that was ruined right from the beginning. Actually, she'd married him with the idea of making a soft easy life. A rich daddy. And a bad mistake.

She really wasn't a cold-hearted bitch, as some people considered her. At least, Virginia didn't think of herself in that way.

It had been a desperation play, to get away from the cheap bars and saloons, to have an easy existence. But daddy found out about her little extra affairs and blew the whistle—and the marriage, daddy and money went down the drain, after five rotten years of living with a man who couldn't give her half the thrill she wanted.

Ed was right. She had to cool it.

Her breathing was heavy and hot. Damn Ed. He could have done things for her—he could have given her a quick one. Something to ease the tight pain which was torturing her.

Damn Eddy! Damn him to hell!

The fury built, then ebbed. A calm replaced it as she reached for the compartment door and opened it.

❋FIVE❋

It was morning, a hot, tropical morning, and Steve was still exhausted. Sleep, when it finally came, had been restless. He'd found it impossible to keep his mind from churning. The sight of Virginia coming out of the pilot's compartment had been just too damned much. His imagination had filled in all the details. Vividly—too vividly.

And the clearly imagined picture was too much. He looked at Virginia and thought about that lush body going wild, springing to life under his caresses. There was such hot fire in her eyes and every movement she made radiated wanton desire being forcefully contained—just barely.

The others were still sleeping when he silently jerked up out of bed and automatically eyed the bunk where Virginia was sleeping.

She seemed to be the kind of female who enjoyed the excitement that her body caused in men. But he was getting the impression she barely controlled an inner raging desire, which was like a continual volcanic eruption.

Steve shook his head, determined to break this train of thought, and turned to the morning's activities.

Some hours later, after a quick breakfast, everybody dressed and readied themselves for the trip ahead. Steve armed himself with the small .38 snub-nosed revolver, which he kept for emergencies. After getting together the necessary items for surviving in the jungle, canteens, and other required supplies, he blew up the large inflatable life raft and dropped it into the water below the pontoons of the plane.

He turned, reached up to the plane's door, and said: "I'll help you down, Virginia. Just take it easy."

His hands touched hers. It was their first actual contact, other than the seemingly accidental ones the night before when the woman was getting another drink. The touch was so damned sensual that Steve felt a wave shoot over him.

The woman surged down against him. The weight of her body, which pressed as if attempting to be as intimate as possible, pushed Steve back.

For a moment he hung there, gripping the woman tightly to him in an effort to regain his balance. He was aware of falling, aware of her body against his and the pressure of her soft, yielding form. She wore shorts, revealing beautifully shaped thighs.

Then it happened. No matter how hard he tried.

They turned, slipped slowly, then all at once cold water folded around his body.

Still the woman clung to him. Desperately holding on, her legs flush against his.

They were sinking deeper and deeper into the icy water.

Steve was a good swimmer, and wasn't worried about any danger involved. The woman still clung to him, and the build up which had burned his nerves the night before, his imagined feeling about her willingness to play serious games through to the end, all mingled together to cause him to do one of the craziest things he'd ever attempted.

She was so close, clinging, soft, wet, her arms and legs twining with his. It was too much to take.

He tried to kiss her as they sank in the water, as the weight and movement of their bodies drove them further and further down. As if guessing his desire, her head moved and her lips eagerly found his wide open.

He had a brief thought of the novelty and insanity of what they were doing, the unexpectedness of it, the wet texture of her mouth.

Then suddenly the kiss slipped, their movements stopped, and their bodies twisted around. His lungs felt near to bursting. The madness washed away and sanity returned.

Steve broke from the kiss and kicked with his legs. He made a powerful stroke with his right hand, driving their bodies upwards. A moment later the fantastic dream shattered as they broke the surface.

Virginia laughed loudly, wiping the water from her eyes. Her hair was dripping wet, plastered to her face and head.

Steve reached for the pontoon of the sea plane and then pulled Virginia and himself over toward the rubber raft.

Ed Blondall was already in the raft; he helped Steve in. His face bore a look of amusement and something else, which Steve couldn't make out.

As the two men helped Virginia onto the raft, Steve couldn't help noticing the naked shape of her breasts under the clinging, dripping cloth of her white blouse.

What the hell, didn't she know what a bra was for? He wondered, actually annoyed. Probably knew, but didn't need one. She had amazingly full, firm looking breasts.

Then their eyes met, and her smoldering look was full of intimate promise of a follow up of that underwater kiss under better conditions when things could be totally explored and finished off to their mutual satisfaction.

At least that's how his mind read the glint in her eyes.

Trying hard to keep his hands from shaking from the effects of that wild impossible kiss, Steve turned and picked up one of the paddles and started the yellow raft toward the shore which was only a short distance away.

A few moments later they were standing on dry land.

Virginia made a big issue of shaking herself off, a display meant to be eye-catching. And both men watched in delight.

"God! That's something!" she laughed, brushing herself uselessly. "I'll never get dry!"

Steve laughed, more from nervousness than anything else. "The sun's hot."

"So am I," she laughed back. "But I'm still wet all over!"

Ed Blondall pulled out a high-caliber rifle from the raft as Steve secured it to a tree near the shore.

"Well," Steve said, "which way to the lost city of Akiki? I take it you folks know what you're doing?"

Ed turned to Virginia. "Don't you think he

44

should stay here...to watch the plane?"

The woman frowned. "We might need help getting through the jungle. Don't you think?"

There was a long silent stare between the two. Ed shrugged, finally. "Whatever you think."

She laughed. "Well, I don't think it makes much difference either way, do you?"

The conversation seemed a secret communication between the two. Steve felt awkward and out of place.

Ed shrugged again, and his eyes moved to the rifle in his hands. "No, I don't think it makes much difference. Only time will make that difference."

"What the hell are you talking about?" Steve blurted, suddenly suspicious.

Virginia laughed. "Nothing, love!"

She moved close and took hold of his arm. "After that little dip, I want you close. To *protect* me...some more!"

Ed Blondall gave them a nasty look and turned away. He pulled a piece of paper from his hip pocket and studied it for a moment. He glanced around the surrounding cove, then walked away for a closer look.

Virginia looked up into Steve's eyes, longingly. She leaned close, whispering in his ear. "I liked it. I liked it really...liked it!"

Her hips pressed closer to accent the obvious meaning of her words. Just in case he was too dumb to get the obvious meaning. Or, perhaps, just to make a hot little joy out of that wonderful contact.

Annoyed more than he liked to admit, Steve gently pulled away from her. They stood a foot apart, but it didn't really make much difference. The point had been made. Her eyes were saying that she hoped their closeness, their kiss in the water, would be only a beginning.

But of what? He wondered, furiously trying to drown those images away.

Ed's voice called out to them. "Come on. I've found the way. Over there—"

He pointed to a clump of green underbrush which was speckled by multicolored flowers. "Through there. We'll find a game trail and then a small brook. Follow that into the hills. It shouldn't be too far."

They started off, Ed in the lead. Virginia walked between the two men, swinging her hips in a fashion, which Steve found fascinating. He wondered how long it would be before Virginia really went after him. If she did, she'd get what she was obviously interested in. It wouldn't be very long before they found a moment for another kiss, and then...

The thought excited and worried him. There was Ed Blondall to contend with. And he kept remembering that the man was almost surely Virginia's lover.

That smelled of trouble. In fact, Steve was wondering if it hadn't been a mistake to get involved with Virginia. There was something strange about these two, but he hadn't smelled it until after they were in the plane—and then it was too late.

Steve fingered the gun strapped to his side. It was damp.

He cursed himself for not having stopped at the life raft and checked the gun.

Then he considered the heat, which was beginning to throb down upon them like a thick, burning

46

blanket. Sweat was already beginning to pour down his face. The gun would dry, but it would need cleaning, and fast.

They entered the jungle by way of a path that had recently been cut and widened, but not enough to remove the branches, which now hit his face and shoulders, legs and body. Insects swooped down to attack any uncovered portion of his flesh.

He heard Virginia curse and slap at an insect on her leg.

"Damned bugs!" she moaned, slapping again at her shapely right thigh.

Steve laughed. "That'll teach you! You should've worn clothes that covered you more, instead of trying to be so bloody sexy!" The words blurted out before he could think them over.

Virginia turned, her face bright with delight. "You honestly noticed! How wonderful! I was thinking maybe you didn't find me all that hot a…lady."

"How could I help it?" He was about to say something else, but a branch whipped at his face, and he ducked just in time.

It was impossible to see clearly for more than a few feet through the thick undergrowth. By keeping his eyes on Virginia's fanny, the movement through the jungle was much easier to take.

Tropical birds sang and chirped; the chattering of monkeys sounded from the trees around them. It was like something out of a Tarzan movie. Beneath the underbrush, the ground was matted over with dying leaves and branches. They inched their way along. The path seemed to wind, turn back on itself and curve around. They had made so many turns that Steve had lost all sense of direction.

What was worse was the fact he'd been totally focused on watching the woman's behind just twitching with every step.

"How far is it?" he shouted.

Ed cursed, then said, "You'll find out."

After a moment, Virginia spoke softly, "Not too far, from what I saw on the map."

Steve had seen the island from the air. He would have thought they could have crossed and re-crossed it by now.

Suddenly they came to a stream, and Ed halted.

"Up this, and into the hills, until we come to the ruins," he roughly pointed in the direction of the stream.

He started off again without a backward glance.

The small stream was thickly surrounded with foliage as it curved around rocks and large, twisted trees. The three kept close to each other, within sight.

Suddenly, without warning, Steve heard a hissing sound—half growl, half moan—from a tree above them and just in front of Ed Blondall.

All three looked up, startled, paralyzed. A black and snarling leopard, his eyes gleaming hatred, was crouched in the tree, looking down at them.

Two things happened almost simultaneously:

Ed raised his rifle; the leopard leaped at him.

❀SIX❀

Sometimes events take place so fast that it's almost impossible to know for sure exactly what happens. Yet, at the same time, everything seems to freeze—motion, breath, life.

Steve saw what happened as though in a crazy haze or a maddening flash of movement, yet it seemed to take forever.

The leopard moved like a raging engine of hate, flashing down from the overhanging branch. Ed's gun spit fire, exploding in a blast that seemed to reverberate and echo again and again.

Man and animal met. There was a pause at impact, then the two tumbled over and over, twisting.

Virginia covered her face with her hands and turned away in horror.

"God, oh God!" her scream rang out in the jungle.

Steve tried to move, tried to think of something he could do to save the man. Regardless of how he might feel about Ed Blondall, he wasn't about to stand by and see another human being cruelly cut to pieces by a savage jungle cat.

It didn't occur to him that a leopard had no business on a Pacific island. All he could think about was saving the man's life.

Then, just as suddenly as the event had started, it was finished.

Both man and animal froze, gasped, sighed, and then collapsed into silence.

Steve already had his revolver in his hand. Now he leaned close to the leopard, aimed the gun and pulled the trigger. The hammer clicked. Cursing, he pulled the trigger several more times. Nothing. Then he remembered his little dip in the ocean and the uselessness of his gun.

He searched for the rifle and found it lying on the ground where Ed had been when the leopard made its attack. Picking up the weapon, he repeated his efforts to make sure the cat was dead. An explosion sounded; the animal jerked and came to a final rest. Kicking it aside, Steve knelt down over Blondall.

The man's right shoulder and chest were cut and bloody and there was a long gash on the side of his head. But quick examination revealed that the man seemed to be all right, considering.

Virginia leaned over Steve's shoulder. "Is he…"

"Alive. A couple of scratches—nothing more. I need something to clean his wounds."

* * * * * * *

Everything happened so fast that Virginia didn't really have time to think. The instant Steve made his request, she reacted. Almost thoughtlessly she ripped at the top of her blouse.

The instant she did that, a voluptuous thrill raced through her!

Oh, what'll he think, she marveled with pleasure, realizing that a very large expanse of naked flesh was now revealed. She was half-topless. *Just let him feast away!*

The first alarm, the first terror, was vanished. Ed was safe, hardly hurt. She moistened the torn piece of cloth and gave it to Steve.

He said: "Unconscious. Will be probably for some time."

He moistened the man's lips and forehead and washed some of the cuts exposed by the ripped shirt. Virginia watched, fascinated.

She'd never before seen a man who had been hurt in this way. The sight of the blood, the excitement of the leopard's attack, left her with a strangely off-beat feeling. She shook it aside and watched Steve.

They were, for all practical purposes, alone. The thought intrigued her.

Ed moaned, but his eyes remained closed.

"He'll be all right," Steve announced some time later, after he had cleaned the surface cuts. "That whack on the head knocked him out. But, with a little rest—"

Steve sat down next to the bole of a large tree.

His shoulders heaved and his chest expanded. "That was a close one!"

Virginia wanted to laugh, wanted to sing and dance, and felt funny because of it.

Her eyes turned to Ed Blondall.

She tried to feel sorry for the man, but no feeling touched her.

Why? She wondered.

Maybe it was because he didn't really mean a damned thing to her. Maybe because she hated him for not having given her a good quick loving the night before. Maybe because she had never really liked him for anything much more than a pleasurable moment.

No man had treated her that way and lasted long. No man turned her down for any reason. Vanished. Good-bye and gone!

Her eyes turned to Steve. The excitement that had flushed over her at the close call they all had had, built another excitement through her.

If only she could strip all the way down to the buff and totally seduce this man ...what a delicious treat that would be!

Virginia laughed suddenly—a loud, piercing, almost insane laugh. She threw her head back; her hands rushed to her torn blouse, which was now making no effort at all to hide her breasts.

Steve leaped to his feet, moving so fast that she was startled with his attack. He grabbed hold of her shoulders.

"Virginia, snap out of it!" he yelled.

Then, with the laughter, sudden emotion flooded through her. A new, surprising emotion, because up to this moment she had felt nothing but excitement at what had happened. Now the tears came, and the laughter raised several notches and became a piercing scream.

She was aware of something hitting her face, aware that her head was rocking from side to side.

Then, all at once, Virginia froze. Her voice choked off. Her throat, raw and hurting, constricted as sobs trembled softly from her lips.

The man pulled her close to him, and she found herself crying uncontrollably. Terrible, aching, convulsive sobs shaking her body.

Her mind was plunging into some ugly pit of emotion, churning deeper. All she could think of now was the man lying on the ground, hurt. She trembled and the tears ran down her cheeks.

Death had almost taken all of them. They could be dead, right now.

How long she hugged Steve Floyd, Virginia didn't know. She sobbed against him, hardly aware that he was a man at all. Then suddenly the awareness grew—the subtle, hot awareness.

Finally she drew away and wiped her eyes with the back of her hand, trying to smile. "I'm sorry. You'd... you'd be surprised what...what was going on in my mind. I don't know what came over me."

For the first time in her life Virginia was ashamed of herself. She tried to argue that it had been a moment of hysterical madness brought on by the close call. But somehow she couldn't believe it. Every time she tried, her mind would argue—you want him. Like mad you want him. Because he's something new—a man—something new. And your body burns like hell for a man—any man, right now.

Steve kept checking Ed Blondall, wiping his cheeks, his forehead. He looked up at Virginia a couple of times, but it was a long while before he actually seemed to notice that she didn't have much covering her breasts.

Standing, Steve stripped off his shirt, revealing a set of hard, full-bodied muscles.

"Here, Ginny," he said, handing her the shirt. "You'd better cover yourself before I forget to act like a gentleman."

She took the shirt. "I guess you're right." She

put the shirt on, and couldn't resist adding: "But how do you know *I* want you to be a gentleman with me?"

"Does it matter?" he countered, looking pointedly at Ed. "This is hardly the time or place to be playing games."

He was right about that. Teasing and flirting like they had been doing the night before was one thing. This was another matter completely.

Virginia wanted to tell him that she didn't give a damn. Any other man would have gotten such a remark, but she hesitated with Steve Floyd. For some reason she didn't want to shock him, to turn him off, to make him consider her nothing but a cheap tramp, a slut in heat willing to toss her body into any man's arms. He could think what he liked, but as long as she didn't act like one, she wouldn't be one.

Her time would come, and sooner than he thought. When that happened it would be the right time, place and setting.

Suddenly Ed Blondall stirred and moaned. They both leaped forward. Steve patted the man's cheeks, gently, but firmly enough to snap Ed to awareness of his surroundings. His eyes flickered and then opened.

It took a moment for his eyes to focus, Then he moaned again.

"Better take it easy, Ed," Steve said. "You took a spill."

After a second Ed nodded.

"Close," was all he said.

"We'll set up camp and rest here for the rest of the day and night," Steve announced.

There was a momentary flicker of fire in Ed's eyes, as if he were about to put up an argument. Then he sighed and nodded slightly. "Maybe...maybe it's better. Where's Ginny?"

"Right here," she said automatically, but her mind was already somewhere else. She was thinking about the afternoon and night. Ed would be asleep, and she'd be alone with Steve. The possibilities excited her, especially since Ed was in no condition to do anything for the cravings of her body.

The wicked, unrelenting female in heat was beginning to rage over her mind, taking more and more possession of its more reasonable parts.

Oh, what they could do in this setting, she mentally thrilled.

"I think we should consider going back," Steve said. "You might need a doctor."

Ed's face grew stubborn. "No!"

"Is it that bad, do you think?" Virginia asked, getting seriously concerned. After all, Ed had saved their lives.

Steve shrugged. "Maybe not. I just thought I'd suggest it."

He frowned and then stood and moved away in an effort to make it possible for Virginia to be alone with Ed Blondall.

GOLD LUST, BY CHARLES NUETZEL

✸SEVEN✸

Steve was painfully aware of the situation. The sight of Virginia was just too much.

Ed had fallen asleep a little after Virginia had gotten through comforting him. In the meantime Steve had gathered wood and started a fire. They had set up their little camp on the edge of the small stream, which they had been following through the jungle. There was little room, little cleared space, but enough to make things comfortable in a cramped, cozy little way.

Virginia had gone around a curve of the stream to take a bath a few minutes before. The sun was getting low on the horizon. Steve was organizing what little supplies they had carried on their backs and was getting ready for a quick meal when suddenly he heard a screech from Virginia.

He jerked up, startled.

Then she screamed his name. "Steve!"

His gun popped out of its holster. It had been cleaned and oiled by now, and was ready for instant use.

Steve leaped to his feet and rushed toward the sound of Virginia's' voice.

The scene he came upon was startlingly provocative.

Virginia was standing almost knee deep in water, facing in his direction, and her body was completely nude. As he rushed up to her, she threw her arms around his neck and hugged tightly against him.

"What happened?" he cried, searching the surroundings.

The woman made a little sobbing sound in her throat.

"The bushes.... They moved.... Something's in them!" she choked out.

Steve disengaged himself from her; painfully aware of the feelings she had caused to surge through him. He carefully stepped to the bushes she had pointed to.

A quick examination revealed nothing. Steve turned to find Virginia standing beside him.

A lump choked his throat.

God, what a beautiful sight. She looked even lovelier in the glowing sunset, outlined in golden flashes of light. Her eyes looked into his openly, honestly aware of the situation. Her lips, full and glistening, were parted.

She stood there, so close that she was almost touching him.

The desire burned up through him like a volcano that had held back its pressure for too long and was about to explode. He felt the needling ache through every nerve of his body.

Virginia leaned closer, a seemingly involuntary action.

Then suddenly they were embracing, kissing hungrily. A tremor broke over them.

"Oh, Steve..." she moaned, gripping his shoulders with her delicate fingers. The desperate, pleading light in her eyes begged with him.

Then their lips met again; this time there were no holds barred, nothing held them back, nothing which even implied that they would stop or that they had done something impulsive. This was for keeps. Very calculated by each of them. There could be no turning back now.

No words, no excuses, no shy statements about not being able to help herself. Virginia was a female whose desires had raged beyond control, and it was obvious that she was desperately needy for a total climatic union.

As she clasped her hands behind his neck and drew him towards her, a voice cried out in the jungle evening.

"Ginny. *Ginny. Ginny!*"

They froze, like two kids caught in the act by their prudish parents.

Steve was trembling, every nerve cursing that other man whose voice had jarred them cold in each other's arms.

But Virginia tensed and surged against him, attempting to cover his lips.

"No. No!" he mumbled, fighting down the almost irresistible urge to ignore the call of Ed Blondall,

"Ginny...Ginny..." the voice chanted like some devilish cry from Hell.

Steve jerked away from her. After all, this was somebody who was a friend of hers—and probably her lover.

Everything seemed weird. Crazy.

"You'd better go—go find out what he wants!"

Savagely he turned and started to walk away.

"Steve," Virginia moaned. "Damned!"

"Yes, I know," he assured her in a trembling voice. "Damned!"

But not right now...because of that damned bastard! He added to himself.

* * * * * * *

Virginia looked down at the delirious Ed Blondall, hating him with every nerve in her. His cry had come out of a fever, and it was necessary to keep a constant watch over him, wiping his face, seeing that he remained covered with blankets. She and Steve were taking turns tending him.

Automatically, almost angrily, she wiped the man's sweating forehead. Then she looked at Steve Floyd where he lay near the fire, his eyes closed, his breathing even.

She wondered what dreams he was dreaming—if any—and whether they had anything to do with her.

Lighting a cigarette, she took a deep drag and thought about the bottle of liquor that they had left back at the plane. How she could use a drink right now.

Virginia got up and went to sit beside Steve, looking at the solid strength of his chest muscles.

He's a strong man—a wonderfully built male animal.

She remembered the frantic pleasure of his body as they embraced. She thrilled to the memory; her hand reached out to caress his chest.

He didn't move.

60

Taking another drag on the cigarette, Virginia toyed with the idea of waking him.

Curse Ed! She'd planned it so beautifully.

Taking a bath, stripping, waiting for a logical time, and then screaming. It was so simple. It could have worked out exactly as she'd planned, if it hadn't been for Ed.

A moan sounded from Blondall and she turned, noticing that he'd shoved the covers from his body.

Virginia sighed, got up and covered Ed, then sat down beside him. She ignored Steve Floyd, not daring to look his way.

Her feelings had simmered down finally, and now she knew it would be a mistake to push too hard with Steve. She couldn't help thinking that he wasn't the kind of man who would take to a girl being too forward. It would work out naturally enough, given time. Assuming they had time.

Virginia rubbed her arms and whimpered silently. Her eyes turned to Steve again.

No, this wasn't the time. Maybe a little later in the night. Maybe!

* * * * * * *

Steve was lying very still, thinking, half dreaming. He had been aware of Virginia sitting down next to him. The touch of her hand on his chest had sent a needling tingle through him and it had been only with effort that he'd controlled the muscles of his body.

Maybe he was acting like a damned fool, but it didn't seem right, ravishing her while the other man was delirious. What had almost happened a few hours before had been something else, something which was out of control. He could rationalize that.

He tried to turn his thoughts away from Virginia and think about something else.

It was some time before his mind saw the image of Linni, the half-caste, who had come to his hotel room the day before. She was a cat, too. But she didn't compare with Virginia.

There was that damned woman again!

There was something strange and almost foreboding about Virginia Donovan. He couldn't get it out of his mind. No matter how much his nerves cried out to embrace her, he kept thinking there was something dangerous about her—something that was hidden, kept secret. Lurking in the shadows. He didn't like the implications in the least. More than once he had been tempted to call the whole thing off before the situation got too sticky. By now, though, it was too late to do anything but run with the punches and make the most of them—the best of it.

To take her in his arms, the moment he got a chance and devour...

Steve felt that once Virginia had received the love she wanted, it would be pretty easy for her to wrap him around her thumb, to completely control him. Some women were like that. They got their hooks in you and it was hard to dig them out. Still, a woman like Virginia...that was one hell of a prize package!

It was a long time before sleep clouded over his thoughts. And it seemed only a moment before he felt a gentle touch on the shoulder.

Virginia looked down at him, smiling.

"Time for a break. I'm bushed," she said.

Instinctively he raised up and their lips almost came into contact. Then, just as the woman seemed about to move closer, Steve leaped to his feet and moved toward Ed Blondall.

There was a long silence. Then finally Virginia said, "He's out. Been out for a long time, Steve."

He turned and studied Virginia.

How easy it would be to simply step over to her and take that lovely form into his arms and let things happen—let things take their natural course.

No, his mind warned. *Don't get involved with this woman. Don't fall under her spell!*

"You'd better get some sleep," he said. He paused. "I think we should call this thing off—for the moment."

Virginia frowned.

"If anything happened to Ed, it would be too late to do anything to change it. And he might be seriously hurt," Steve warned.

The woman came to her feet and moved over to him. Her face was tense with emotion.

"I won't turn back. Don't try to make me!" she warned.

"I think we should head back, the moment he's out of the fever!"

"I don't give a damn about that. He'll be all right. And he wouldn't want to turn back. He has too much tied up in—" Her voice broke off as her hand covered her lips.

"What was that you said?" Steve demanded, instantly alert.

"Nothing."

"Damn it all!" Steve cursed, gripping her arms. "Tell me what you meant by that!"

Her eyes were wide with alarm, her lips open, and her breath short and choppy. "Please, Steve. Please. You wouldn't understand."

"Try me, or it's finished right now. Money or no money!"

"Please, Steve...please...please," she begged, the entire time leaning closer to him. "Steve, this means a lot to me. A terrible lot. You have to accept things. I'll cut you in for a lot more money. Make it five thousand. You'd like that, wouldn't you?"

Without warning she pressed against him and raised her lips to his. He responded for a moment, then, realizing what she was doing, he forcefully shoved her away.

"Virginia, what the hell is going on?" he demanded, angrily.

Without warning the woman tore at the shirt she was wearing. Steve's shirt. Two buttons popped off it as she jerked the shirt away from her body. In another moment her shorts dropped to her feet and she stood defiantly before him.

"See if you can resist this! Let's not argue, Steve. Let's finish what we started," she pleaded, her eyes blazing. "I can't take it any longer...wanting you!"

And before he could do anything, she threw her arms around him and hugged tightly to him, covering his face with desperate kisses.

❋EIGHT❋

There are moments of complete insanity when all logic goes out the door, where intelligent action is impossible.

Steve knew exactly what he was doing; he knew that what was happening was going to get him burned, and good. Blistered, burned, barbequed, and staked out like a helpless piece of meat. He was literally helpless.

But this lush, wild offering was something no man could possibly turn down. She made it impossible for him to reason, to be logical, to do anything other than respond without rational thought. And after that, there was only sensation—sensation that wrapped around all consciousness, all. Awareness. She literally encased his whole being within her eager embrace. The endless chasm of her closed him in a fiery vice of soft hot flesh. She sobbed and moaned in delicious pleasure as they rode higher and higher on one wave after another, drowning in their mutual pleasure. Pleasure that raced faster and faster to total ecstasy.

Later, like coming out of a bottomless pit, Steve moved away from the still form of the woman.

He slowly stood, as if she were some kind of hellish demon, stunning and confusing and totally irresistible

He turned and moved toward the stream, trembling, exhausted

What the hell had come over him? What was happening? It was like some kind of nightmare from which he couldn't wake.

Never had he experienced anything like it, or even dreamed it. But then, he had never really met a woman like Virginia Donovan.

Richly dangerous, completely powerful. Some kind of super-woman, a super-sensual creature to damn men and tempt them to their doom.

To hell with her. He'd kick the whole show off the road.

Feet padded behind him, He turned to find himself facing a delighted, happy, wonderfully excited face, which beamed up into his eyes.

"Oh, Steve. God. Oh, Steve. You're wonderful!" she moaned, throwing her arms around him. 'Wonderful!"

He tried to find the words, tried to say them, tried to tell her to go to hell. But the longer she held on to him, the more impossible the words became. Words choked in his mind.

"Steve, I've never known a man like you before. I need you more than anybody in the world!" Then her lips caressed his ear lobe.

Damn her. No man could convince himself that a woman was lying when she said things like this, no matter how much he realized it was all a line designed to get the exact effect it was getting.

All at once Steve realized that no matter how stinking the set-up was he would go along with it. If for no other reason than this woman. She made a man totally helpless. He knew it would happen again as sure as he was breathing. And he also knew about the danger that lay in wait for him if he played the game for a second time. Every logical thought, every nerve, told him to back off now, before it was too late.

But another voice convinced him that it was already too late.

Their lips met. Steve's thoughts whirled. It was much like being possessed by some other being, controlled completely by an outside force. Steve knew that now she had control, knew that the questions he had wanted to ask would be unimportant.

Like a man who needs his dope, Steve allowed himself to be controlled, allowed, himself to fall into the trap which she had opened for him. And when the trap shut, he felt an almost strangely wonderful sense of relief. Right or wrong, he was committed. No fence riding. He was in deep and all he could do was sink or swim. The rule was simple: survival.

But in her arms, for him, it was total submission without any conditions.

What happened from here on would be the outgrowth of their actions now.

As they locked in an embrace, Steve even forgot to think about the situation, the danger, and the thoughts, which had been in full bloom only an instant before. They all blurred into a red sensation. He was barely aware of the excitement of Virginia's nearness, which continued to demand his total being. She was like a furnace, raging out of control, a lava flow that simply washed over him again and again.

GOLD LUST, BY CHARLES NUETZEL

❋NINE❋

It was early the next morning when Ed Blondall moved and opened his eyes. Steve, who had been keeping watch over the man, jerked to attention.

He leaned over and touched Blondall's forehead.

The fever had dropped away. The man felt cool.

Ed looked up at Steve. For a moment, neither of them said anything.

Steve grinned. "You had a close call."

The man nodded slowly, attempting to rise up.

Steve helped him to a sitting position.

"I think we'd better consider turning back," Steve said. "You had a close call, and—"

Ed Blondall groaned and shook his head. "No dice. I'll be right as ever..."

Virginia woke then and moved over to them.

"Feel better?"

Ed nodded.

"Strong enough to continue?" Her question was tense, controlled.

"I think so." Ed checked over his body, feeling the wounds that cut his flesh. He grinned and then stood, shakily. "I'm starved."

Steve gaped at the man, unable to believe his eyes. "You sure you'll be okay?"

"I'll be fine!" Ed snapped.

The next half-hour was a revealing one for Steve Floyd. After what Blondall had been through, he would have thought it had to mean the end of their little trip.

He pointed that out to the other two, but Ed quickly announced, "I'm going on. If anybody has any other ideas, they can stay back!"

"What's the hurry?" Steve pushed, determined to find some answer this time.

"None of your business. You were hired for a certain job—nothing more! You do what you're told, and that's it. Understand?" Blondall's voice was threatening.

Silence. Then Steve nodded. But mentally he told himself to be careful of their every move. For the first time he was completely convinced that there was more to the situation than either of the others were about to tell him at the moment. Perhaps other dangers to avoid.

"Okay," Ed said a little while later, after they had finished their breakfast. "Let's get the hell out of here!"

The man checked his rifle while Steve helped Virginia gather their supplies. It was at this time that Virginia whispered in Steve's ear when they were far enough from Ed so the man couldn't hear. "I'm worried about him."

"Why?" Steve whispered back.

"That look in his eye. Did you notice?"

"I've known him for a long time. It was...*frightening!*"

Then she moved away.

A little later they were on their way along the

70

stream, toward the more hilly territory where the lost ruins of Akiki lay waiting.

* * * * * * *

Virginia was pleased with herself. She had managed to hook Steve, and keep him hooked. More than that, she remembered the private times with Steve with great delight. Now she had something to fall back on in case things went too sour between her and Ed. The idea was somehow very inviting.

To Virginia, this whole thing was a chance to get on top in the world, to be in such a situation as to never have to worry about anything again. There was only one thing she didn't like about it. It was impossible to trust anybody, completely. She was tied to Ed Blondall, but if a man like Steve were with her, it might be possible to change things. It gave her an Ace. And that could make all the difference in the world.

All other thoughts concerning what was happening just bubbled behind a mental wall of resistance. There was a part of her that simply didn't like anything she had become in the past years. Some of the decisions she'd made were false runs, mistakes. Some were stumbling moves for momentary survival. But every step had taken her down a pathway that now seemed seedy and undesirable. But escape from the trap of a loveless marriage was one thing difficult to find undesirable. Cheating on her husband hadn't been a first choice solution. It was merely a result of nature. She needed a man. Her body craved sex and even more than that, she craved being near somebody who might care. She

was empty inside. It had been far too long to remember what it might be like to actually be loved
and cared for. Had she ever really know that kind of
love?

The hot sun was playing down on her and she
felt the sweat squeezing from every pore. Her throat
was like a desert, and it was necessary to keep sip-
ping from the canteen at her side.

The bugs and insects kept swarming around her,
but she'd become used to it by now and merely
swatted them away.

The urge to strip and give her body the full free-
dom which nature intended it to have was held back
by only two points: one, the insects, and two, Ed
didn't know yet that anything had developed between her and Steve. And it might just be better to
keep that quiet, for the time being. Otherwise, a part
of her might have enjoyed running around naked,
openly teasing the two men.

That was an evil thought, yet thrilling. It was the
kind of game she enjoyed—having two male animals fighting over her. What a delicious thought, in
fantasy, maybe, but certainly not in realty.

It was an exciting idea. But she really didn't
want somebody getting hurt.

Games were one thing; cruelty another. Virginia
didn't consider herself a cruel human being. Even if,
at times, she'd been wickedly cruel about teasing
men with her body. That was harmless fun.

It seemed, to her, that the island was an endless
trail leading them nowhere. The night before had
been a series of strange and different experiences
for her. In Steve's arms it had been wonderful. But
when she was alone, the sounds coming from the

dark, foreboding jungle had been too terrifying. She'd held the rifle tightly to her, frightened. Now, in the heat of the day, it seemed different—and endless.

She wondered what would happen when they got to the ruins and found her ex-husband. Steve would immediately know what was happening, and he might turn. That was a chance they had to take.

Ed had the rifle and a pistol, too. Enough to overpower Steve.

Plus her own relationship with the pilot.

They had planned, in the beginning, that the pilot could be overpowered and forced to do what they wanted and her idea had been to use her sensuality as another kind of wedge.

She hoped that Steve would prove easy to handle.

Oh, God she hoped he wouldn't prove difficult. She really liked him...maybe too much. Too damned much!

They were coming to a curve in the stream. Ed, a little ahead, suddenly gave out a yell of surprise.

Virginia rushed forward, and suddenly found herself facing the outer fringes of a crumbled ruin.

GOLD LUST, BY CHARLES NUETZEL

✸ TEN ✸

The city had been quietly waiting for hundreds or even thousands of years. No man on earth knew how many years it had been waiting and watching. Perhaps it was silently aware of those who came to rob it of the treasure which its long dead builders had cast in their religious zeal to worship the virgin, the perfection of womanhood, and so to curse all who might defile that perfection.

It was a city of silence, having seen splendors, of which only it might know, and might speak of, if it but had a voice to do so.

It was a city of quiet, which had sunk into a shambles, a mass of sorrowful broken rocks and incomplete walls, giving only a hint of its one-time glory and beauty. Here and there was the silent voice of a statue to speak of what once had been; what a long dead artist had once created with his fingers, his mind and his soul. A silent, dead memory of what had once been.

And in its secret stomach, carefully hidden in a dark chamber in the heart of the city, waited the golden statue, the idol, the Virgin, who waited for all those countless ages, quiet and alone. And the Curse lingered in the darkness, maybe alive, maybe supernatural, and maybe nothing more than all curses, mere empty vocal words wafting on the tropical breezes.

She had been a patient Virgin, without thought, without voice, without passions; but sparking, creating, fanning passions in the minds of men in her ancient time, so long ago. And within those inspired passions lay the danger, the curse which threatened all, which also sat silently waiting—written on the base of the Virgin, carved in symbols which none of the present world could read, none had read or seen for maybe centuries.

None, except, perhaps, the dead man lying at the base of the statue. But he wasn't about to talk, either, for his voice was stilled by something more deadly than a simple curse. And yet, maybe because of the curse. A small stone dart was caked with dried, brown blood, and was deeply embedded in his back.

* * * * * * *

Steve came to a stop at Virginia's side. What he saw was haunting, beautiful, awe-inspiring.

All he could think of was of how this had been built hundreds or thousands of years ago. How many people had loved, hated, lived, struggled through their years of life, and then died in this place?

All gone. Not even memories were left. Just these stones to remind modern man of what might have existed. Yet they had been human beings, with souls, with dreams, with hungers and need that had driven them through life. And then their civilization, culture and people who had simply vanished as if they had never been.

Life was so frail.

In reality, there wasn't all that much to see. Just the indication of what might have been—what had been, much too long ago to have any recorded way of truly knowing. And all of this, on a small island in the middle of nowhere. Maybe the island had once been much larger; perhaps it had sunk slowly into the sea, hiding all but this portion of an ancient town, city, and citadel. Was this simply a part of the whole, which had disappeared from visual sight above water? Was there more out there on the ocean floor? Was this simply an inner temple? Or was this all that had ever existed?

Would anybody ever know the truth, now?

The jungle thinned out into volcanic rock and then leveled to reveal the remains of what once was a fairly good sized city—considering when it probably had been built. Considering what wasn't evident.

Considering everything, none of which made any sense at all.

Had some alien civilization come down out of the skies and located a colony here? Creatures from across the galaxy?

Hardly. That didn't make sense except to fantasy nuts.

Steve decided to just roll with the punches. Take in what was there to see and not try to explain what couldn't possibly be explained.

The suggestion of a wall circled the ruins. Just here and there they could make out a raised portion where a wall had once been. How tall it had been, there was no way of knowing. Too little was left.

Beyond that was rubble; broken rocks; half columns; stumps toppled over; sides of walls, which must have been dwellings of some kind. In the center of all this was a pyramid-shaped structure which was in far better condition. But even this was sadly lacking in detail. The centuries had taken their toll, leaving only the tantalizing suggestion of what had been.

Steve had heard the strange story about the lost continent of Mu, which was supposed to have been in the Pacific Ocean, and the Motherland of all mankind. According to the story, Mu was, perhaps, the Biblical Garden of Eden. The legend had it that a large and expansive civilization had developed on it, spanning most of the Pacific coast of both North and South American, and of Asia and Africa. It told of how the people of Mu had settled the lands and how, over time, the continent might have erupted and sunk below the Pacific Ocean, leaving only its mountain peaks. The theory claimed that this legend gave reason for the practices developed by the peoples of these Pacific Islands and it explained the statues on Easter Island, which had been a mystery for centuries. Supposedly, many of the people of Mu had gone up into the mountains, and when the continent sunk, they survived.

Nobody in their right mind or with any kind of education gave much strength to the theory of the lost continent of Mu. Science had rebuked it. Yet many people who believed this, claimed that "where there is smoke, there is fire".

And standing right before them was nothing short of raw "fire" to smolder the mind and excite the imagination.

The sight of the ruins before him smoked Steve's thoughts and excited his imagination.

Could this be something of what was left of Mu, the lost continent?

But of course, that was quite impossible.

Everybody loved to believe such stories, and they loved to see evidence like this and point to it as being proof.

But, in the end, it always turned out that another explanation was more likely. Here were the ruins of a small, apparently highly-developed culture, which had survived on this lost island which had been given the name of Akiki. The ruins were known, surveyed and ignored. The curse, which had been handed down from father to son over the centuries, had cooled intense interest in Akiki.

The fact that some explorers had searched for the Virgin Idol earlier and had ended up dead, lost, or never heard from again, had discouraged much investigation. But all this was mere supposition and raw superstition—primitive and native.

And the white man, the scientist, just hadn't gotten around to paying much attention to this island and what it offered, aside from a casual exploration.

Steve had read a book on Akiki some years back, written by a man who claimed to have visited the city with a party of scientists. The book and the short exploration had satisfied the scientific world, for the time being, at least. The conclusions were merely that some race of people, who had been fairly well advanced, had developed a culture which had disappeared centuries before. Some talk had been made about starting an excavation of the ruins, but no native help could be had, no funding available and the expense didn't seem justified. Scientists ignored the legend of the Virgin Idol. The island, the ruins, and the legend were all interesting, but written off. A mere localized legend, a pathway to nothing worth serious investigation at the cost of such expeditions.

Except for some fortune hunters, since the disappearance of the last party to do any investigation on Akiki, nobody had come here for either scientific reasons or treasure hunts.

But what impressed Steve more, in a depressing way, was this ancient civilization—all those people. People who had, at one time, existed here. And now they were gone. They built this great city; they lived in it, they loved, they survived, and they died. Now, the only things left to show for their lives were these ruins. We live for a moment, then we are dead and forgotten. These people once believed in their own gods. They had believed in their own gods, their own rights and wrongs. How different were theirs from today's gods worshipped by modern man? And were they as real and as powerful? Or mere illusions? Nobody would ever know. And now it was practically all dust, left to our imaginations of what had been and now was no more. How small it made everything seem now; how unimportant; how shallow.

A man's life is but a speck in eternity, a fraction of an instant. The universe is vast and endless, both in time and space; a flicker, a blink of an eye between the beginning of this ancient city and the present-day moment. Yet millions, billions of people had lived and breathed during that entire short instant in eternity.

The full impact of all this shuddered through Steve Floyd, dwindling all things, including himself, down to a speck of nothing— an unimportant mortal. He could feel the change coming over him, as if some hand reached out and touched all that there was of him.

He had lived in the sorrow of the lost love, his wife. He had let his own life slip and fade away. And yet there seemed to be a strangely perverted beauty to what he had done in the past. He had lived—maybe for the wrong reasons—a life, which was full, in a strange way. Primarily bumming, but it kept him sheltered away from the tug and complications of civilized life, free from the grind that now, at the site of Akiki, was of no real importance. The responsible person held down a sound job and went to work every day until retirement came to finish off the last days of his life. Responsible people created empires—real and imagined.

But they all crumbled away.

Even Rome had finally fallen. But that magnificent empire had, no doubt, risen, long after this city at Akiki had once thrived and then crumbled.

And it hadn't mattered in the least.

Suddenly a new perspective shadowed over him, over every thought, every action.

Responsibility was to each person a means of surviving the best that they could. Responsibility was taking life and living it fully. Responsibility was not hurting others while cutting a personal territory of happiness. And more importantly, so-called social responsibility came in different packages for every civilization, every culture and every time frame.

Out here, time was frozen.

To live and let live, to experience, to seek out the pleasures, which have meaning to you, and make the most of every moment, was truly the responsible thing to do; no thoughts of right or wrong. For, in the end, all things will crumble to dust.

The world, as humankind knew it, would vanish. The planet would burst into stardust when the sun exploded in its final stages. And who knew what would follow that?

Shaking himself, Steve forced his senses to the immediate surroundings. His eyes moved to Virginia Donovan, and a feeling of excitement choked him.

What a lovely woman! What a beautifully exciting woman! This was the kind of female who was worth fighting for, worth living for; worth loving.

Well, she was certainly quite a bit above the native women who had serviced his male needs these last years.

He felt totally confused concerning his thoughts about Virginia. Male hormones were raging all too easily at her visual image, coupled by the sharp memory of what her body had done to him.

Ed Blondall's voice broke the long, hypnotized silence that had fallen over them.

"Well, let's find Donovan!"

Virginia roused herself, as if coming out of a daze. She turned, looking into Steve's eyes. There was a strangely pleading expression, which reached out to him as if silently asking for forgiveness of some kind. But that didn't even make sense.

Then she shrugged, her form dancing under the man's shirt that Steve had given her.

"I guess so," was her reply to Ed. "About time we find out the truth!"

He asked, taken aback at her statement, "What truth?"

Virginia hesitated, and that 'look' clouded her eyes again. "We'll know...soon enough."

It was a starkly vague reply, avoiding a direct answer. And, without question, it was all the woman was about to say about the matter.

They started forward, slowly, carefully, walking past the shallow ruins of the wall, into the first portion of the city of Akiki.

Steve felt totally out of sorts, unsettled by Virginia's response to his question and by the general moods and attitudes of the other two.

Somehow it seemed impossible to think that the woman could want to hurt him. Ed was another matter. He decided to be very careful and watchful around him.

Instinct warned him, once again, as it had earlier, that something was terribly wrong about this whole trip; something dangerously wrong.

GOLD LUST, BY CHARLES NUETZEL

❈ELEVEN❈

Ed Blondall felt a surge of strength move through him as he stepped forward toward what he knew must be the temple in the center of the ruins. Here, somewhere, would be the Idol—deep inside. They knew only that the Idol Chamber was in the temple.

His body was covered with sweat. The throbbing ache, where the leopard's claws had done their work on him, had weakened his nerves and muscles. Now, with the treasure only a matter of yards away, he felt excitement building up over the pain, numbing it away.

His muscles tensed; his fingers hardened on the rifle. The next moments would tell a lot, would settle the course that the trio was going to take from then on. The minute they came upon Ralph Donovan, Ed planned to put a bullet in the man's body, before any possible difficulty could come from that direction. And the moment that happened, Steve Floyd would have to be contended with.

A thin cruel smile curved on Ed's face as he waited for the moment of action. It was going to be a pleasure to put the flying champ in his place. He hated men like Steve Floyd, but he never really understood why or even tried to reason it out. Ed

Blondall had always moved and acted for the moment. The thrill of the unexpected, the thrill of making others bend to his wishes, was enough to make all this worth it.

Ed could easily guess that something had probably happened between Steve and Virginia. The woman needed men too much. Virginia wouldn't have ignored the opportunity, which his own unconsciousness had created.

And what was more, he hadn't missed a trick since regaining consciousness. There were those subtle glances, the suggestion of hidden intimacy. Ed was sure something had been going on between those two. And that, alone, was going to make it easy to start the muscle stuff on Steve when it became necessary. In fact it would be a pleasure beating the man senseless, then placing a foot right into his groin! Stomp it hard, violently, and see the anguish rip through those smart-ass eyes. Oh, it would be delightful giving him some real working over before putting the bullet between his eyes.

They came to a stop in front of a large opening in the pyramid. It was a stony, hard-surfaced structure, marked heavily by time. The ground around the temple entrance was packed hard, higher than it must have been when it was first built, as the centuries piled the land high around it.

Footprints would have been hard to see even if they had been made.

Ed ignored the fact that there was no evidence of anybody there. He turned and faced the other two.

"We'd better have a look-around."

Virginia nodded.

"How about shooting a gun?" Steve offered. "Isn't that the fastest way?"

Ed nodded.

"Well?"

Raising his gun, Ed pulled the trigger a couple of times. Then, just for kicks, he aimed it at the top of the pyramid, at the remains of a stone face, and fired. The bullet slammed into the stone, chipping away a portion of what was left of the nose.

A long, loud silence followed, almost deafening. Ed realized what a noise the birds had been making, up until then.

Laughing, he turned and looked at Steve. "Well, doesn't look like anybody's here!"

His eyes snapped to Virginia's. "I wonder where he is?"

"In the temple?" Virginia offered.

Ed nodded, eyeing her appreciatively. What a sight. What a woman...

Then, irritated, Ed turned his eyes toward Steve. Somehow he would have to make certain that the man got out of his way. He could use a little privacy with Virginia. It had been quite a while—before the departure for Akiki—since this urge had hit him so strongly. Of course there was always a way of getting Steve to leave...return to the plane for something. Anything.

Shrugging, Ed twisted around and faced the temple entrance.

"Flashlight?"

Steve stepped forward.

"Here we go," he said, and started to step into the temple.

"Hell, hold on, buddy!" Ed warned, pushing up

beside Steve. 'We don't know what's beyond our next step. I've heard something about this place."

"Superstition!" Steve announced. "After this many centuries there couldn't be any danger!"

"Maybe you're right, but let's be careful." Ed was thinking about the possibility of coming face to face with Ralph Donovan. His finger tensed on the rifle's trigger.

"Okay," he announced. "You can go first. But keep close. And not too fast!"

Virginia stepped in behind Ed as they started into the darkness of the Akiki temple.

✱TWELVE✱

Steve felt a sense of creepiness settle over him. The only thing he could see was what the flashlight revealed, which wasn't much. Some of the light flared off reflecting on the walls.

They were going down a narrow hallway with stone walls, ceiling and floor. The stones had been cut into about two foot blocks, and fitted carefully together. Age, time, and centuries had stained the rock blocks into a dirty gray, splotched with green. The passageway dipped downwards and then without warning forked off into two passages.

They stood there for a while and then Ed said, "The left one, first."

Steve aimed the flashlight and then started down the left corridor. They hadn't gone far before they came to a dead end.

Turning, Steve flashed the light in Ed's face, starting to suggest that they turn back. The other man cursed and abruptly slammed his rifle against Steve's hand.

"Damn you!" Ed screamed.

The flashlight clattered to the floor and blinked out.

Steve froze, ready.

He could hear the sound of breathing. Virginia gasped, sobbed.

"That was a smart thing!" Steve snapped angrily, wanting to choke the life out of Ed Blondall.

"You startled me!" Ed said.

"Virginia, you have a flashlight in your pack. See if you can find it." Steve's voice was tight and cold. He would settle accounts with Ed Blondall a little later, Steve promised himself. Right now wasn't the time to complicate things.

The sound of the woman looking for the flashlight seemed to take forever. The darkness was oppressive, closing in on Steve.

Ed moaned, "For God's sake—hurry!" There was panic in his voice, sharply edged, high and near the point of cracking.

Finally a beam of light cut into the darkness. Virginia pointed it back along the way they had come, and they started walking toward the fork.

Ed was breathing hard—so hard that it sounded as if some sighing monster were trapped in the corridor with them. When they reached the fork, he cried, "Let's get out of here for a while. I need some air!"

He grabbed the flashlight, and Steve saw him tear it away from Virginia's hand. Then the man started down the corridor that led outside the temple.

There was nothing to do but follow him.

The moment they were outside, almost blinded by the sun's light, Steve pushed up to Ed's side, grabbing his right shoulder and whipping him around.

"You ever do anything like that again and I'll

make you eat that gun!" Steve snapped, squeezing hard on the man's shoulder.

Ed moved so fast that Steve was off balance, unprepared for the sudden attack.

The man's left fist jerked out and smashed into the pit of Steve's stomach. Before it was possible to recover, Steve felt something explode at the point of his chin. The world toppled and darkness slammed shut around him.

* * * * * * *

Virginia gasped in surprise and fear. The look in Ed's face frightened her as he turned away from Steve.

"That's it! The dirty bastard!" Ed cried, kicking a booted foot into the other's side. "That does it up good!"

Leaning over, Ed pulled the .38 revolver from Steve's side holster and stuffed it in his own belt. "No more trouble from fly-boy!"

"You can't—can't leave him this way," Virginia said in a small voice. "You don't think he'll cooperate if he's—"

"Just shut up, Ginny. I know what I'm doing. It's better this way, anyway. It had to come to this. Hell, what do you think he'd have done when he discovered the truth? This just makes it easier. Now his teeth are pulled."

"But we can't both watch him!" she pointed out.

Ed laughed bitingly. "Oh, I don't think there's any trouble about that. One of us can always be around to see to it that he doesn't run off and leave us alone. In fact, maybe it would be better to bundle him up, securely—so he can't run off."

Virginia shook her head. "Why don't you put the gun back? Unload it. Then he'll never know. And if things get...well, complicated." She shrugged.

Ed nodded after a moment of thought. "Okay. Okay! That's pretty good!"

He grinned broadly as he took the .38, opened the cylinder and dumped the bullets into the palm of his hand. Then he replaced the gun in Steve's holster.

"No sense getting him too dangerously suspicious. When we get back to the plane, then we can do things up big. A gun at his back will make him do anything we tell him!" He chuckled and looked at Virginia. "Now let's go find out what happened to Ralph! He has to be here somewhere. We can search the... Wait. This bastard... We gotta play it safe for a moment. You watch him. I'll give a quick search. Tell him I'm sorry—anything you want, just so that he understands."

Ed moved away and Virginia knelt down beside Steve and tried to revive him.

"Steve. Steve," she said, patting his face, shaking his shoulder. It was some time before he showed any signs of reviving. Finally his eyes fluttered and then opened.

* * * * * * *

It was a while before he realized where he was, or what had happened last. He looked up into the woman's eyes and for a moment contentment soothed him. Then he remembered.

92

'Where the hell—"

"Steve, he's gone to search for Ralph," she said quickly. "He's in a terrible rage. I'm frightened."

Steve sat up, rubbing his chin. He smiled crookedly. "What the hell did he hit me with?"

"The rifle. It was horrible," she moaned, her face drawing tight.

Virginia looked away. "I'm sorry I got you into this." Her eyes closed, as if attempting to blot out an image. "I've lied to you right from the beginning. It wasn't my brother I wanted to find; it was my ex-husband. And Ed … he threatened to do something violent if I didn't play along with him. I found out where Ralph was going—and we followed. The rest is true—but Ed plans on taking the idol and having it melted down—for the money. I'm afraid of him. He said to tell you that he was sorry, so when he comes, let things ride."

The woman looked at Steve for a moment. "Your gun. He unloaded it."

With that Virginia stood and walked away, not facing him.

Steve quickly checked the gun and reloaded it. His mind was in a whirl. What Virginia had told him fit in with most of the facts. He just wondered where she had fit in. It was simply impossible for him to believe that she wasn't after the money, too.

"Steve?"

"Yes?"

"I want the money. I'll split it with you," she offered. "Ed plans on killing you."

For a moment Steve hesitated. Then on impulse and inspired by the fact that he was in the middle and outnumbered, he said: "It's a deal...if things get messy!"

She turned and was suddenly in his arms.

"I was hoping you'd be that way. Maybe if we told Ed...maybe he'd go along with it all."

Steve nodded. "Maybe we should just play it safe. Wait and see what happens."

Virginia snuggled closer. "You mean a lot to me, Steve. I'd do anything in the world for you."

Steve only grinned to himself, fully aware of the final trap, which had nearly sprung on him. He now knew that he was walking a thin line between life and death. He didn't trust Virginia as far as he could throw her.

In fact, Steve realized, he had to watch out more for the woman than the man. Ed Blondall had declared open warfare—even if indirectly. Virginia was surely playing both ends against the middle.

He shuddered, realizing the full implication of the situation. The only way out was by playing along with the dangerous and impulsive woman in his hands—and he doubted that she wouldn't blow it all up in his face. Only one other chance was open to him—return to the plane and leave the others behind. It was the one thing that neither would give him the chance to do.

❋THIRTEEN❋

Ed Blondall searched quickly around the ruins and found what was left of a small camp. From every indication there had been only one man in camp.

He searched through the few supplies puzzling over the fact that there hadn't been other members in the party. He had automatically assumed that Ralph Donovan would have had others with him. The small tent in which Donovan must have slept had a cot and small damping table. It was on the table that Ed discovered a diary.

Hurriedly he opened it. A short examination of the pages toward the last revealed some startling facts that he would never have guessed.

Chuckling to himself, Ed slammed the book shut and then sat there, thinking over what he had learned.

Ralph Donovan had come to the island alone, and for very good reason. The fact that he had a very good theory about where to look, made it easy to assume he would find what he was looking for without any help.

Ed stood up, put the diary in his pocket, then hurried back to where he had left Steve and Virginia.

"Well," he said, coming to the others, "I found the camp. Deserted." He turned his eyes toward Steve." I'm sorry about that."

He noticed the flicker in Steve's eyes.

"Sure. We got a little nervous—okay?" Steve offered, extending his hand.

"And I'm a little under the weather anyway."

After they had shaken hands, Ed said: "We might as well attack the temple. But first, I want to tell Virginia something. About her ... brother. Do you mind?" he asked Steve.

The other man hesitated just long enough before saying, "Sure."

Steve walked about twenty yards away.

Ed turned to Virginia. "I found something interesting. Your ex was broke! Imagine that!"

Virginia gasped in surprise. "You must be kidding."

He pulled out the diary, opened it and handed it to her.

"This good enough for you, Ginny?"

Virginia looked at the neat handwriting that she immediately recognized as her husband's.

The entry was dated a month past. It read:

> I found the way into the lower chambers today...it's just a short matter of time before my accounts are settled. When I think about all the money that's merely a stone's throw from where I now sit, an excitement takes control of me that...but it's worth all the effort it's taken. Now, once I get back, nobody will be aware of the mess things have

gotten into. The Idol is supposed to be worth a million or more...and it should be, from what I saw of it. Tomorrow I'll make a further examination. It was too late last night...and danger might lie there, secretly hiding, to spring to life after centuries of being buried...there's that curse...best to watch out...a curse that was supposed to protect the Idol.

Though it seems incredible, after such a long time, that any booby traps could still be working, it's just not worth taking a chance.

Ed said: "Turn back a page...read that." Virginia did so.

I'm sure I'm close to finding the way into the inner chamber. It's going to take some doing—but I've covered almost every square inch. I managed to at least get into the inner shell. The passage to the right. I wasted a lot of time finding out which way. But now it surely can't be further than a few feet and a few hours of work. Thank God I know exactly what I'm doing.

My only regret is that I can't turn it over to the proper authorities. Ruining such a work of art is a criminal shame. But the fact remains that I need the money—all of it—or go to prison...

Virginia looked up and saw that Ed Blondall was grinning. "What's so damned funny?"

Ed chuckled. "Just think—the old fool was just as crooked as the rest of them! And we were thinking he was the holier-than-thou kind of ass. Probably cheating on his investors. Be easy for a man in his position. You know how he used to play the stocks."

Virginia nodded, and felt a pang of guilt, not knowing why.

"I feel sorry for him," she said in a small voice. "He always seemed like a nice sort under all that obsession of his...when he was young, maybe even a good lover...I wonder what's happened to him."

Ed shook his head. "He wouldn't have left the camp. So, I guess we'll find out when we do a little serious investigating. I saw a large oil lamp at his camp. That'll give us more light."

"Do you think...think he was killed...by the—"

"Curse?" Ed grinned. "By some foolishness! No doubt. Carelessness, no doubt. And probably lucky for us, too!"

"What about Steve?"

"What about him?"

Virginia thought quickly. "I told him half the truth about the set-up. He swallowed it. Why not play it out— in the open? It might make things easier. When the time comes, that'll be a different story."

Ed frowned, then he finally nodded. Slowly the frown opened into a big grin. "Ginny, you're tops. I'd never thought of playing it that way. But, considering how things have worked out, I think you deserve a big...medal!" But the look in the man's eyes was saying something completely different. His eyes were hot as they looked at her. Then he sighed. "Okay, let's fill our partner in on the deal—all be old buddies—and then take a look for that inner chamber. And the gold!"

With that, Ed turned and called Steve Floyd over to them.

GOLD LUST, BY CHARLES NUETZEL

✹FOURTEEN✹

Steve Floyd felt like a man trapped between two charging lions, without any escape other than hoping that the lions would miss him and encounter each other in their vicious fury. Of the two, Virginia Donovan was by far the most attractive choice. But she was also the most dangerous. She played both ends against the middle—he was sure of that. And with that body so easily seductive, it would be easy to twist both Ed and himself like little puppies right between her breasts—if that's what she wanted.

As he listened to Ed Blondall's offer, it was hard to keep down the gnawing at his gut level. He couldn't understand how two people could be so damned cold-blooded about money and life.

"...We get the Idol and I have a place where I can turn it all into hard cash!" Ed was announcing with a grin on his face. "I understand that Ginny told you the score."

Steve looked at the woman, and there was just the flicker of amusement in her eyes.

With either one, if he trusted them, he'd end up dead, in the middle of nowhere. Right now, all he could guess was that they both needed him. They needed each other for the time being.

A nice little trio.

He was the only one who didn't need either of them. He was, too, the only one who could get them off the island—neither of them knew how to fly a plane. That was his ace.

"Okay, then. Let's go back into the temple and find out whether the Virgin Idol is there," Steve suggested.

Ed's eyes narrowed. "I'm calling the moves, Mr. Floyd. And don't you forget it!"

Steve shrugged.

The two men glared at each other and then Blondall made a motion with his rifle. It was the kind of gesture that a guard might make toward a prisoner. Steve pretended not to notice, stepped forward, took the flashlight from Virginia's hand and went toward the entrance of the temple.

His only ace was the fact that Ed Blondall thought his gun was unloaded. But Virginia knew all the facts and could throw in with whomever she wanted. The woman was playing a clever game.

A dangerous game.

Blondall called to him. "Wait. I forgot the lantern."

The man turned and moved off around the edge of the temple.

Virginia quickly came close, slid her arms around Steve's neck, and snuggled close to him. "I was afraid you'd blow it."

'What's the game now?" Steve moved her gently away and looked into her eyes.

"Be careful and play along with Ed. If anything gets...dangerous, we can take over. After all, Steve, you have the plane. There's no reason we should cut it three ways, is there?"

"You know where to take the Idol—for hard cash?"

Virginia's face hardened. "No. But don't you?"

Steve quickly nodded. "There are places."

"Well then? We won't need him, after the Idol's on the plane. Will we?"

The sound of Ed Blondall returning cut off their conversation. The man was carrying a lantern, which he lit and handed to Steve.

"You do the honors!" he ordered.

Steve moved into the darkness of the temple's stone corridor.

This time it was possible to see markings on the stone walls. Endless pictures were cut shallowly into the stone. In many places the markings had worn away or been covered over by the green moss which had gathered over the stones. The smell of rot seemed heavy, and Steve wondered why he hadn't noticed it before. It was an old, dank smell.

Finally they came to the fork, and this time they turned to the right. They hadn't gone more than a dozen yards before they came to a wall that cut across the corridor at a forty-five degree angle. At first Steve believed it was a dead end, then he noticed that the wall was actually some kind of door. The right side revealed a dark opening.

Ed shoved Virginia back to Steve's side. "That old bastard must have had a devil of a time finding this!"

Steve nodded.

"Want to do the honors?" he offered with a thin smile.

Ed shook his head. "Your privilege…"

There was no doubt in Steve's mind that the

other was playing it safe. If any clever traps were in evidence, it wouldn't be Ed Blondall who fell into them.

Steve put his shoulder against the wall and it opened slowly, but with amazing ease.

Raising the lantern high above his head, he peered into the chamber beyond.

What he saw caused a gasp of surprise to tighten his stomach muscles; air gushed from his open mouth.

The room extended for about twenty yards in front of him, and what seemed like the same distance from left to right. In the middle of the wall opposite was an altar, and on it a small statue stood, shining in the dim light of the lantern. The statue wasn't more than three feet tall, but its obvious value, glittered before their eyes. Gleaming stones were set over the golden statue of a nude woman, whose arms were stretched out as if in offering. The eyes were flickering diamonds, the breasts were starred with what looked like rubies.

Ed Blondall pressed against Steve's back. Steve was about to take a step forward when his eyes instinctively lowered.

But not in time.

His foot moved down into emptiness. Then the world seemed to twist around.

The next thing Steve knew, he was falling downwards through empty space. An instant later the darkness had exploded in his brain, leaving a sense of complete defeat.

* * * * * * *

Virginia screamed in the darkness. The walls seemed to be closing in on her. For a long time the panic held her, then finally she realized what had happened, and that there was only one thing they could do.

The sound of Steve's body hitting water had sent terror through her. For a moment she'd seen him drop, then fall into the large pit that stood between them and the altar room,

Ed Blondall was moaning, sobbing. His voice held a note of hysteria. "We'll die...never get out of here—never get out—"

"Ed! Ed, shut up!" Virginia snapped, returning to sanity. The unexpectedness of what just happened had shocked and frightened her for the first moments; now she felt coolness, which amazed her.

The whimpering stopped. Virginia pulled the pack off her back and fished out the flashlight that Steve had returned to her when he took the lantern.

She flashed the light in Ed's face. His features were twisted into a horrible grimace.

"We have to get to Steve, somehow. Was there any rope—anything in Ralph's camp?"

Ed thought for a moment and shook his head. "I don't know—don't know—"

"Get hold of yourself! We're only feet away from the greatest fortune you'll ever get your hands on!" she snapped. "And we need Steve—to get off this island!"

She moved to the edge of the pit, which began just a foot away from the entrance.

She flashed the light down into the darkness. The pit dropped away for about fifteen feet. For a moment she didn't see Steve, then she saw a weakly moving body floating on the surface of the black water.

"Steve! Steve! Steve!" she cried, again and again. "Steve!"

* * * * * * *

The sense of complete defeat had choked him, fading away as consciousness slipped, then flared up again. He felt his lungs bursting and became aware of coldness squeezing over every muscle.

Then out of the darkness he heard a voice calling his name. Steve moaned, then gradually remembered what happened. Now he was aware of floating in water.

He thrashed around and finally managed to gain some control of the situation.

A light was flashing down into the water, and in its glow he tried to make out his surroundings. The pit was deep—too deep to climb out of. The water was cold. Beyond being completely trapped, though, he seemed in one piece. His forehead ached where it must have hit the side of the pit in his headlong fall.

"Virginia?" he gasped weakly.

"You okay?" she answered.

"I think so..."

"How long can you stay there?"

"Forever, I guess," he said ironically.

"We'll go outside and try to get something to pull you out! You'll be all right?"

"All right. But hurry..."

Then the light flashed away. For a moment he saw its glow reflected against the high ceiling. Then he was in complete blackness, alone, trapped.

How long could he thrash in the water before exhaustion took its toll? He fought back the threatening terror as darkness crushed into being.

Then he thought about the walls of the pit.

Swimming to his left, he reached out and found the smooth surface of the wall. At the water level it was worn away, but a few feet higher he felt the broken surface where the rocks were laid close together. There was barely a finger hold—but enough. He searched blindly for a better hold, but found none. The idea of climbing out was thus eliminated. But at least he'd be able to stop treading water while he waited.

Then, slowly as some slithering serpent winding its way around his body, he felt the cold, chilling terror of the darkness creep into his mind. The whole universe was without light, for this was his whole universe.

He tried frantically to think about something else. He tried to picture Virginia's face, her lips, and her body.

Yes, he told himself. *That's it. Think about Virginia!*

Her soft form clinging to his, heir hungry lips...

Yes, that was the only thing holding back his insanity!

Virginia—her arms around him, begging for more; Offering. That, was the most beautiful thing he could think of right then. The one thought making it possible to wait here. He mentally focused on her lush, passionate body.

What the hell is taking them so long? Are they going to leave me here?

Oh, God! Help me!

It seemed like he'd been in the icy water forever. Minutes were hours. The darkness closed in
tighter.

What terrible creatures were hidden in this
nightmarish darkness?

The panic moved up a notch. His fingers tightened on their narrow hold. He hugged the wall in
desperation, seeking safety in something solid.

Then his feet felt a gaping hole in the wall beneath the surface. Water gushed beneath him.

A scream rushed from his trembling lips. It
sounded against the walls of the pit, winding upwards, bouncing against the walls of the chamber
above him and returning louder to his ears.

Then another calmer voice told him to relax and
try to think logically. Slowly the scream died and
his mind turned onto another track.

This was obviously some kind of trap set up for
the protection of the Virgin Idol. Water fed into the
pit from this opening in the wall. There was probably another on the other side.

Steve realized that the only way to hang onto his
sanity was to keep busy, to keep his mind on something besides his situation. Slowly he moved along
the wall, searching for the other opening, the one
designed to take the water out of the pit.

For a moment the panic threatened again, then it
subsided. When he came to a large opened area, the
fear rose again. Then he forced his mind to wonder
about it, to question. The opening was cut into the
wall at water level. A passageway seemed to lead
into the pit. His imagination filled in the gap. No
doubt they put some kind of reptile into the pit,
where it would make quick work of anyone who fell

into it. It was a guess, but in the guessing Steve managed to keep his fear buttoned down and away from his conscious thoughts.

What the hell was taking them so long? He moved around the circumference of the pit. Finally he came to the water outlet. Steve stopped, tried to relax, and then moved back to the opening. He had begun to accept this as the place where some man-eating creature had entered the pit. The opening wasn't large—just big enough for some crocodile to move along. He pulled himself so that his shoulders were wedged against the small opening, his head forward. There he rested, fighting back the fear. Terror kept threatening his mind.

He tried to think about the civilization, which must have built this place. *What kind of life was it being a member of this kind of culture? Life must have been cheap.*

His thoughts blurred and ran out of shape.

The darkness seemed to close in again; he realized that the soft whimpering sound was coming from his own lips. The sound began to grow louder. He forced himself to think about Virginia again.

Then, a voice screamed into the darkness:

"Where are they?"

He knew it was his own voice screaming. It seemed to be controlled by some other will.

He screamed again and choked on the scream, swallowing it down.

They were going to leave him there, forever. Forever...

He heard the sound of footsteps coming toward the pit. At first he believed it was his imagination.

Then a voice called down.

"Are you still there, Steve?" Virginia asked.

❋FIFTEEN❋

They managed to find a rope, but it was attached to the tent and it had taken time to strip it away. Now, leaning over the pit, Virginia watched Ed lower the rope.

She held her breath, afraid the rope might not be long enough. She directed the light into the pit. It dimly reflected upwards.

Steve's voice cried out in relief: "Have it!"

Both Ed Blondall and Virginia held tight to their end of the rope. It took their combined strength to keep from being pulled into the pit with Steve. Virginia had no idea just how much help she was to Ed, but she knew enough to hold tight. That even a little extra amount of tension on that rope could make the difference between success and failure.

Finally the flyer pulled himself up over the rim of the pit. Breathing hard, he lay there, dripping wet.

For the first time in her life Virginia felt a wild emotion of caring move through her. Her mind was screaming over and over again. *Thank God, Thank God!* But what amazed her most was that the emotion was more than mere relief over getting their pilot back in one piece. The man was beginning to mean something more to her than just a means of getting off the island.

Her mind insisted: *What the hell's happening to you?*

"Okay," Ed said harshly, "Let's find some way around the pit!" He took the flashlight from Virginia and pointed it towards the edge, circling around its circumference. On the right was a narrow passage. "The bastards were smart!" he acknowledged.

Steve, still breathing hard, managed a weak comment. "I thought you guys weren't going to make it."

"You scared me," Virginia admitted, reaching through the semi-darkness and touching his shoulders. An electric thrill shot up through her. It was the first time, for quite a while, that her thoughts had turned to any physical needs. And with the thoughts came a yearning to be held in Steve's arms, to be kissed, loved, caressed. She shook down the desire as Ed's voice sounded harshly.

"Come on!"

Steve fell in beside Virginia, but Ed blurted out, "You first!"

Virginia said: "And get him killed?"

With that she started to take the lead, but Steve pushed past her.

"It's okay," Steve assured her. "I'll be more careful this time!"

He started along the narrow walkway and into the chamber of the Idol.

* * * * * * *

With each step a chill of fear worked down his spine. It had been a close call, but now that he was aware of the danger, he moved carefully. It was only a stretch of five feet, then he was in the chamber.

Ed Blondall was carrying the flashlight. The beam flicked across the room and Steve jerked to a stop so suddenly that Ed bumped into him from behind.

"What the hell!" Ed cried, seeing the same thing that had caught Steve's attention.

"Ralph?" Virginia gasped.

They moved toward the body stretched out in front of the altar.

Steve was the first to see the small stone dart in the man's back.

"Careful!" he warned. "God knows how—but this place is still set up and dangerous. Look!"

He pointed to the dart as he leaned over and carefully turned the man onto his back.

"Ralph!" Virginia moaned in a low, sick voice. "The poor fool!"

"He made it past the pit, but..." Steve shrugged and turned to the Idol, now a mere shadow in the darkness.

Ed Blondall said: "Let's get the damned thing and get out of here!"

"Oh, you're welcome to, if you want a dart in your back," Steve offered.

Ed chuckled. It held a strange threat. "You do the honors, Steve."

Steve turned, but couldn't make out the face behind the flashlight, which was pointed at him.

"Go ahead. There's a rifle pointing at you!" Ed snarled.

"So. Now we start playing it honest!" Steve's spine chilled again. "I thought it was partners. And how are you going to get off the island?"

Virginia sighed. "Can't you two act logically? How many booby-traps could this place have?

"Look at Ralph's hand—it's stretched out. He must have touched something which set off the..." Her voice faded.

They were silent for a long time. Then Steve spoke, calmly and clearly. "We could do a little investigation first. Virginia, take the light. Ed and I can check around carefully. Flash the light on the statue."

It was a moment before Ed handed the light to the woman.

Steve moved cautiously up to one side the statue, looking at the small figure.

It was perfectly crafted. He had never seen anything so beautiful in his life. The body itself was delicate, young, the breasts high, pink tipped by ruby stones. The arms reached out, as if pleading for love. The eyes had an imploring expression. The lips were parted slightly in the ageless symbol of desire.

He was amazed, looking at the golden figure, how the Virgin Idol resembled women of his own day. It showed how little mankind had changed in the centuries since the image had been made.

The gold was dulled by the centuries, but all in all, the statue was in amazingly good condition. At the base, where it was set in stone, a depression showed where one of the carefully fitted stones had been placed. It didn't take much guesswork to realize what had happened. No doubt that was the trigger. When Ralph Donovan had depressed it, accidentally or by design in an attempt to remove the statue or pry it loose, the trap had sprung. The revenge, planned ages ago, had reached out to inflict its sentence on the man who dared to rob the tomb of the Virgin Idol.

How could it be possible, after so many ages, that the spring—or whatever method was used—would still be in working condition? Surely there could be no other booby-traps.

On impulse, Steve stepped to one side of the statue and reached for it. He grabbed it by both hands and tugged, attempting to lift it from its base.

The statue held firm for a moment, then lifted. At the same time there was the sound of rock crushing against rock. A warning of impending danger.

Steve released the statue and it toppled.

Virginia screamed. Ed cursed. Suddenly, as if from nowhere, a huge stone slammed down from the ceiling. It smashed sickeningly into place in front of the altar, exactly where Steve would have been if he had grabbed the Idol from the front.

GOLD LUST, BY CHARLES NUETZEL

✸SIXTEEN✸

Dust swirled around them like a cloud of angry, vengeful fury from a living demon. Steve choked on the thick, sickening air. For a long time there was complete darkness. Ed Blondall moaned into the silence. Finally the flashlight flicked on, and Virginia rushed to Steve's side

"Are you all right?" she cried, alarmed.

Frowning in concern, she caressed his cheek.

"Fine," Steve assured her in a shaky voice. He took the light from her hands and quickly shot it around the immediate surroundings. The Idol lay on the floor, a few feet away.

"Well," Steve breathed, "maybe we can get out of here."

Ed had recovered. Now his voice boomed in the small confines of the room. "Hurry up. You carry it and I'll follow. From now on, I'm boss! Understand? Both of you!"

Virginia shuddered against Steve, then she pushed away. "Ed, what's wrong? I'm with you!"

"That's what you think, baby! That's what you think!" He laughed nastily.

Steve could hardly repress a grin. Two double dealing people twisting things around and around to suit themselves. At least it gave him a break. It

117

might be easier to combat Ed Blondall than the woman. After that he'd consider Virginia.

Without a word Steve bent down and lifted the Virgin Idol. It was a heavy load, but he threw it over his shoulder like Santa Claus with a bag of goodies, then turned and started for the narrow pathway along the wall and the pit.

Each step was a struggle to keep his balance, but finally he made it into the passageway beyond. Virginia had moved in front of him before he crossed the narrow ledge and now he followed the silhouette of her body, outlined by the beam of the flashlight illuminating the corridor beyond.

The distance seemed a lot shorter now than before; they were blinded by the midday sunlight.

Steve immediately saw his chance.

If he were blinded, then Ed Blondall would be, too.

Steve twisted around as the other man came out of the temple behind him. He grabbed the Virgin by the head and swung the statue at Ed.

Things happened so fast then that it was impossible to recount them later. The Idol made contact with Ed's shoulder, knocking him off balance. Then Steve dropped the Virgin and pulled his gun from its holster.

"Okay, Ed, just take it easy!" he demanded.

Blondall snarled and sprang to his feet, leading with the rifle. The weapon was held like a bayonet, heading directly for Steve's mid-section.

Steve pulled the trigger.

Then he felt the impact of the rifle in his stomach. A moment later something smashed against the back of his head. After that it was lights out. The show was over.

* * * * * * *

Ed Blondall pulled the unconscious flyer to one side, then rolled him over and tied his hands behind his back. Then he turned to Virginia. He had retrieved the man's gun, noted it was loaded, shrugged.

"Smart guy reloaded, then forgot his gun got wet in that watery pit," he grunted, then chuckled.

They stared at each other for a little while. Ed grinned. "Okay, Ginny. I'm sorry I had to pull that gag on you in there. It was the only way to get him off guard."

Virginia blinked. She couldn't believe he actually thought she could be fooled so easily. He thinks she was a dumb one.

She didn't reveal her contempt and disgust, but smiled instead. "We've been friends too long, honey. Anyway, we need each other, don't we?"

Ed nodded. "Right now I need some rest. Flyboy here is taken care of for a while We might as well relax God, it's good to be out in the daylight again. I thought I was going to choke to death in there."

Virginia looked at Steve and felt a pang of regret. Then she turned her eyes to Ed Blondall, who held all the cards but one. He had the guns.

But luck was still on her side, as long as she had a body to dangle in front of any male.

Ed moved into the shade of a crumbled wall.

Virginia followed, lowering herself to his side.

She reached a tentative hand to his arm "Ed. Ed,

it's been too long!"

Ed Blondall's eyes roamed over her and a rasping breath gushed from his lips. The expression in his eyes fired with interest as her hand moved to his chest.

Virginia's first thought had been to overpower him with her offering and somehow slip the gun from his hip. But now she knew what would happen. It would be impossible for her to turn down what he wanted to give her. Her body ached with need, regardless of all they had just been through.

Virginia moistened her large lips with the tip of her tongue. Suddenly her mouth was dry, her hands shaking. She threw her arms around the man, almost sobbing. "Oh, Ed."

His lips covered hers as his arms folded around her waist and drew her tightly to him. The kiss was rough, brutal.

Her thoughts whirled even in the embrace. How different Ed's caresses were, compared to the tenderness of Steve. Ed was an animal who took what he wanted, cruelly and with no thought for the woman. As he was taking her, now. And yet her body, that body which had ruled her for so long, responded. Fully and completely.

She thrilled to the rough touch of his fingers, mauling her breasts, toying with the hardening nipples until they were hurting. His lips sucked on them; rough, crude, savage-like. The sensations that ripped through her were overwhelming. She could not get enough of him. He ran his hand down across her stomach and then clutched at her groin. She almost sobbed when his fingers enter her. She arched up violently against them, gasping in uncontrolled

120

orgasm.

"Oh! Do me. Now!" she muttered so intensely that it came out in a choked voice. Her own hands reached down and brazenly grabbed hold of the thick throbbing hard as she squeezed his shaft. He released her and then he plunged deep inside of her with one swift stroke. She greedily moaned with pleasure. He was like a savage beast, determined to rip through her flesh with total selfish intent. A raging powerhouse of hard muscle, he was ramming at her with almost brutal force, again and again, penetrating like a mad machine bent of total destruction.

And she could only react, respond matching his beat with her own. Her body arched up pushing hard against him to meet every downward thrust, engulfing the wild fury of him totally, as if she couldn't get enough, as if he couldn't be big enough or long enough to penetrate her deeply enough.

It was a cruel, horribly self-centered, and almost destructive taking of one each other. No tenderness, no caring, just harsh demands exhausting every smashing blow of their bodies against one another.

When passion had given way to spent exhaustion, it was like coming up from the bottom of a sea, slowly swimming upwards, until light flickered and then air finally thrust life into her. She turned, conscious of a new emotion. She puzzled over it as she moved away from the sleeping Ed.

She felt some how cheap and dirty.

Her body had responded, yes.

But a subtle change had taken place. An element had been lacking—one thing which she had never really been fully aware of in her life.

Her thoughts kept turning to Steve. Gentle, good

121

Steve.

Things were so different with him...

Virginia finally gave up trying to understand what was needling through her emotions. To hell with men, she told herself, annoyed.

Yes, it would be good for a while with Steve.

But then the thrill would end, and it would be good-bye Steve boy.

She considered their present situation. This was a serious game, with wealth on one side, death on the other. Her best bet was with Steve. Ed would turn on her, the first chance he got.

She slipped over to where Ed was lying on the ground and reached delicate fingers toward the holstered gun.

Just as she was about to touch the weapon, the man reared up like a snake, grinning insanely. His hand slammed out across her face. As she fell back onto the ground, Ed leaped at her, sending another blow to her mouth. Panic and terror ate through her.

"God! Ed! Ed..." she moaned.

The man hesitated, staring down at her tortured face.

"Don't ever try that again!" he warned, starting to get up.

"Do what?"

"The gun!"

"I wasn't!" she snapped, coming to her feet and moving close to the man. "I wanted to come over to you. I was only moving the gun away so I could come and simply devour your body with my lips."

Her arms circled him suggestively. In her mind, Virginia was already beginning to form the plans to kill Ed Blondall. No man had ever hit her before, and he was going to wish to God that he had never done so.

Ed Blondall was rigid for a moment. Then, slowly he relaxed and jerked her tight against him.

"I'm sorry," he moaned, covering her lips with his own.

Virginia put all her acting ability into the kiss.

"Oh, Ed, I love you...I love you—" she moaned.

"You bitch!" Ed laughed, stepping away. "What a woman. I'm sorry about...well, knocking you a bit. I can't take any chances. You can understand that, can't you?"

His eyes gleamed. His face was damp with sweat.

Virginia grinned, shrugged. Then she searched for the rifle and spotted it a few feet away.

Carefully, casually she moved toward it as Ed gathered up his clothing.

She was just in front of the rifle when Ed's voice knifed out, "Don't touch that!"

"What?" she asked innocently.

"The rifle."

"Oh, for God's sake, Ed. This is getting silly." She twisted around, glaring at him. "Either you trust me or we can't be together— how can I feel any- thing for a man who doesn't trust me?"

"Okay, okay!"

As he was reaching for his shirt, Virginia turned again, grabbed the rifle, then jerked around and faced him, pointing the weapon straight at his chest.

For a moment Ed's face remained blank. Then he slowly grinned. "So, you were playing me for a fool, weren't you?"

He started toward her. "Well, well. What do you know about that?"

"Just stay where you are, Ed," she warned, tightening her grip on the trigger.

The man continued to walk forward. "You might consider the fact that there are no bullets in the gun."

"That's too old a trick, Ed."

"Okay, then. Pull the trigger," Ed suggested, still grinning, still walking toward her as calmly as if he were on a street in Los Angeles or London.

Virginia hesitated. Then, when the man was within a few feet of her, she pulled the trigger.

The click sounded in her ears like the explosion of doom.

The gun was empty.

✸SEVENTEEN✸

Then the man leaped toward her. Desperation, the survival instinct of every animal including man, surged up through Virginia. She moved the rifle like a club. How it happened, she would never know. It was much too fast—without thought, without hesitation. She saw the man rushing for her, murder in his eyes, and then she moved.

The rifle lifted in the air and then slammed down, barrel first, into the side of Ed Blondall's head.

For a stunned moment the man stood there, paralyzed, his eyes staring coldly at her. Then she swung the weapon again, once more against the side of his head.

Ed Blondall fell like a chopped tree and smashed into the ground at her feet.

For a few seconds Virginia stood there, stunned. Then, slowly, she released the rifle and staggered back, away from the still form.

What had she done? Her mind screamed. Then a slow grin spread across her face.

Her hands were shaking, but a calm slowly washed over her. *Yes, it had been easy. So easy to stop him, to kill him.*

Virginia went over to where the holster and gun

were still lying on the ground. She picked up the weapon and looked at it.

Then, very coldly, she stepped over to the unconscious man, placed the gun at his temple, and squeezed the trigger.

The gun spat fire; the man's head made a dull, popping sound.

Virginia turned away from the gory sight of Ed Blondall's bloody head, unable to look at what she had just done. A sickness threatened at the pit of her stomach, but after a moment she gained control of herself.

Good riddance! Too bad, Ed, but you crossed the wrong woman. You played the wrong game! You deserved to die!

Virginia moved toward Steve Floyd and bent down over him. She had her ticket out of this damned place and would have enough money to be set up for life.

Steve Floyd would do anything she told him, he would be putty in her hands, like all the times before, like all the other men.

Even Ed Blondall had been fooled, for the most part.

She worked on the ropes binding Steve's hands behind his back, then she struggled to roll the man over onto his back.

The next line of business was to revive him. She went and found the canteen she had carried since leaving the seaplane. A moment later she splashed water over Steve's face. When he stirred, Virginia leaned over and kissed his lips, feeling a sense of excitement in the act.

He moaned and his eyes fluttered open.

* * * * * * *

Steve looked up into Virginia's eyes and for a moment couldn't remember where he was, or what had happened last.

He recognized Virginia and was suddenly aware of her complete nakedness. Her skin against him was soft, damp, and seductive. And regardless of the pain in his gut and the side of his head, Steve felt excitement press up through him.

Then he remembered what happened last. He raised up on his elbows with a jerk.

"What the hell?"

Virginia looked away.

"He's dead," she choked out between trembling lips. Then the emotion-filled words poured out. They sounded like the words of a frightened child who has done something so terrible that it can't believe or accept it.

"Oh, God, Steve, what am I going to do?" she moaned, suddenly facing him and pushing against his chest. "He was going to kill me! I didn't know what to do—after—after he forced me—oh, God, it was terrible. He was never like that before," she sobbed in his ear.

Steve felt a wave of tenderness move through him for this woman. Regardless of what he knew her to be, regardless of how she had planned and obviously used him and Ed Blondall. He couldn't help feeling sorry for her, as he might feel sorry for any woman who has gotten in too deep. No matter what, Virginia was a woman. A very exciting woman. No man could really be blamed for falling

under her spell, or being more than casually interested in her.

Virginia had what it took, physically to get any
man's interest and hold him helplessly in the palm
of her hand. It was easy to feel a sense of protection
toward her.

Caressing her head, Steve became painfully
aware of the woman—aware of her warm nearness.
Slowly the desire started building. He fought it off.
He fought until Virginia's lips found his, covering
them with eager kisses.

"I love you, Steve. Oh, God help me, but I love
you!" she moaned.

But the kisses were those of a frightened
woman, a desperately frightened woman and didn't
generate any real growing passion.

Finally, partly because of the pain in the side of
his head and partly because of the situation and the
sight of the dead man only yards away, Steve
pushed Virginia away from him. He stood, slowly
and painfully.

"You'd better get dressed," he suggested, starting for Ed's body. When he saw the gaping hole in
the man's head, nausea constricted his throat. It
seemed incredible that the woman had been able to
kill him that way.

As he examined the man, Steve felt a nagging
doubt about the story Virginia had told. There were
no signs of struggle on her body. He had noticed
that quickly, but hadn't given it much thought.
There were broken areas on the man's head, as if
he'd been hit by a blunt object.

A shudder rushed over Steve as he realized what
must have happened. Somehow Virginia had man-

aged to knock the other man unconscious. Then, after Ed was helpless, she had blown his brains out.

He turned and was about to accuse Virginia of having murdered Ed Blondall, when he saw the gun which was now strapped at the woman's side. She had pulled on her clothes and was buttoning her shirt.

If Virginia had killed Ed Blondall, what would keep her from killing him?

Steve pondered that for a moment and then decided to play it carefully. Once they had reached the authorities, it would be easy to turn her over to the police, and tell his story. At this point she needed him more than he needed her. She couldn't get off the island without his help.

He spotted the Virgin Idol and abruptly realized what it could give him, what it could offer. It was worth a fortune; could bring enough money to set up half a dozen people for life. An ancient Goddess of love, no doubt. And she had cast a strange spell over everybody within reach.

He turned and looked at Virginia, wondering if it might not be sane, more intelligent, to throw his *lot* in with the woman. After all, she no doubt had been forced to kill Blondall. The man had deserved it—that was damned right! He had deserved to die. Yet Steve couldn't help knowing that she hadn't told the full truth about the attempted rape— if that was possible—and the killing. And therein lay real hard danger.

Whatever made Virginia run was something dark, deeply hidden within her own mind—maybe even she didn't know what was racing that beautiful body.

Virginia came up to him. "Now it's up to you. We have to find a place where we can turn the statue into hard cash. You said you knew a place. And then—the two of us, and the world!"

She embraced him, so ardently that pleasant dizziness welled up over him. Then she moved away, smiling. "We'll be good together, Steve. Wonderful."

Steve instinctively flicked his eyes toward Ed Blondall. He wondered if she'd told Ed the same thing. Virginia Donovan was like a black widow. She devoured her lovers after the last mating. He had to hold back a shudder. The worst thing he could do was to think of Virginia as a helpless woman. She was as deadly as the gun at her hip.

In fact that body was a total death-trap. Once she turned her flesh in as an offering to a man he was simply helpless to submit until she'd worked her spell to totally melt down any resistance or strength left in him. Her passions could fully drain a man. There was no doubt in his mind that the idea of possessing her just one last time was obsessive.

Just one more time in heaven. Or maybe, on this island, a long time together, totally feasting on the altar of lust. He could easily worship her body for a very long time. She was, regardless of anything else, one dish, one hell of a female body to enclose around his whole being. And they were alone on a tropic island, and there wasn't any way for her to leave without his help.

What a lovely image that framed in his mind. Just lost for an unknown time with her willing, passionate body a literal slave to his needs. How could she get away from him? And the way she enjoyed sex, the way her body demanded a man to it to feast hungrily upon, left no doubt about the woman's very basic nature. Virginia lusted for a man like men craved women. Just thinking of spending a lifetime in the virgin place, the two of them exhaustingly devouring one another night after wonderful night was a heady fantasy.

What an illusion that was. What a nightmare, too.

Total nightmare.

How could any man resist being enveloped in her arms and body, just one last time? Just one more time to feast on the lovely voluptuous beauty of this lustful woman.

Whatever drove her, Virginia Donovan was, beyond doubt, one hell of a woman to make love to. And that was the only word he could think of—for it was more than just lusting, just taking some biological treat with a native female, or any other woman he had known.

Some women were beyond mere pleasure, some, like her, were meant to be totally worshipped, totally possessed and taken. But Virginia was more powerful than merely being an object of worship with a beautiful body.

When it came to a woman vamp like her, any male would end up helpless under her spell.

Some women were like a goddess of love. Or an evil demon from hell. Virginia was, no doubt, a perfect combo of both goddess and demon.

And in her arms a man simply didn't give a damned!

Steve Floyd knew just how helpless she could make a man feel. How completely consumed in total obsession.

He wanted her like a drug.

No. He needed her like a druggie needed his next fix.

Steve shrugged and forced a grin to his lips. "Well, we might as well get started."

❋EIGHTEEN❋

The next hours of the long day went by slowly.

They had gotten the map from Ed Blondall's pocket and buried the man. Then they started back to the plane. The map was well marked and easy to follow, as long as they were careful. Virginia carried the rifle, and Steve, the Virgin Idol.

The sun baked down upon them like a blazing flame. The hike through the jungle, even when they reached the stream, was exhausting and nerve-wracking. Every step suggested death and danger to Steve. A leopard, a snake—any jungle beast could reach out suddenly. Only Virginia and the rifle stood between them and that death. And he had his pistol, which he'd cleaned and reloaded.

They had planned to get to the plane before darkness. Steve was sure they could make it. But as the sun slowly slipped lower and lower, it seemed as if they weren't getting any closer. The stream turned and twisted. When the sun had settled over the horizon, Steve finally had to admit the truth. They were lost, confused and must have missed the point where they should have gone onto the game trail.

Darkness fell fast. Suddenly Virginia came to a standstill and turned, her face contorted with fear. "We—we won't make—it. I thought it would—"

"Slow down," Steve warned. "We can't be lost. At least not much, on an island like this. The stream has to go someplace. All we have to do is follow it. Once we reach the coast it will be an easy thing to find the plane. So take it easy!"

All the time Steve's eyes were searching the surrounding brush near the stream. Just around the next curve of the stream he was sure he saw a clearing. He pointed toward it with his free hand. The darkness was almost complete now, and the jungle night creatures were beginning to create their own sounds.

"There," Steve said. "We'll stay—there."

The night sounds of the jungle around them were like a haunting melody, which held the terror of the unknown. Anything could be out there, and their minds played along with the suggestions offered by the darkness.

To Steve Floyd, who had experienced a moment of almost paralyzing terror in the black ink of the Akiki pit, this fear was more easily controlled. All people fear the unknown, the blackness through which only the imagination is able to see. The brave overcome the fear, the cowards become overcome.

He gathered up some dry twigs and pieces of wood and built a fire. In its low blaze it was possible to see their immediate surroundings.

After a warm meal of canned beans, they settled close to the fire in an effort to keep warm against the damp coolness of night. Little conversation passed between them now, but Steve was doing a lot of thinking.

It was an obvious temptation to turn the Idol into hard cash, to take the offering which Virginia's body was willing to give. For as long as it was in her interest to have him as a plaything.

On the other hand, it seemed a damned shame to melt down such an object of art—so beautiful, so perfect. He found himself studying the statue in the dim light. The flickering flames played on the lines of its perfectly shaped body.

What creative genius had shaped this little Idol, this lump of gold, into such a beautifully molded image? He was lost in thoughts about the Idol; lost in a fantasy all his own, trying to picture the culture which had developed the artist, trying to design a man's life from birth to death.

His thoughts were so far away from reality that he jerked in surprise when Virginia's voice cut into them.

"Steve—what are you thinking?" Her words probed at him with that edge of womanly irritation which all females will express when they aren't the center of a man's attention, and don't like it.

"About the Virgin. Don't you wonder about who made it?" he asked, looking up at Virginia.

She shrugged. The action moved her figure under the shirt. The sight taunted him, though he doubted that it was intentional.

"Just think, Virginia. The man who shaped this—he must have been a true genius, a true artist. A great deal of care and thought went into it. Was there a model? Was the model a virgin like this gold; as cold, hard, and unfeeling? Or was she his mistress, his lover? Who knows what stories she could tell—this Idol of Gold!"

"Who cares?" Virginia snapped. "It's a fortune and that is all that matters!"

135

"It's almost a shame to—ruin it. Maybe a collector would pay a lot for such a piece of art."

"And we would have to wait until we find one, and hope he loves it enough? Are you kidding, Steve? Hell, we can't take the chance. What if some government official discovered that they had first rights to anything found on Akiki? What if they claimed it? And you have to think about the chance of some bastards moving it—taking the Idol for themselves. I don't want to take any chances. There's enough money in the metal, in the stones, to set me—and you—up for life. What difference does it make?"

Her words were harsh, and he knew it would be a mistake to be too pushy about the subject. So he remained silent, but his thoughts told him it would be impossible to melt it down, to ruin it. Another morality far surpassed personal gain. This morality said that such an object was more important than money, that it didn't belong to this age or this century, but to all mankind. All ages should have the chance to see and wonder about this marvel—like the ruins of Rome, the Pyramids in Egypt.

"Steve—how long are you going to play with that damned thing?" Virginia snapped in a low, throaty voice.

His eyes moved once again to the woman, and he felt dryness in his throat.

She unbuttoned her shirt and sat there challenging him with her eyes. "You don't know something about me, Steve. I simply have to have physical love. I can't go long without it. I've been this way ever since the first time."

Her hands moved over her arms, her stomach. "I

136

can't play waiting games, Steve. I can't wait forever."

She slid over close to him and her hands slipped around his neck, caressing. "I'm a woman, Steve—a flesh and blood woman. I'm not cold like that statue. I'm throbbing with life, with hungers and desires. Don't you understand?"

The offer was bold and brazen, but the kind which no man could ignore. He wasn't child enough to believe they wouldn't seek out each other's bodies; it had been obvious. Even if the timing seemed strange, what difference did it make? This was his moment to be totally lost in her, to be surrounded by all of her, to be taken into a living ecstasy.

Maybe they could stay there on this island forever...never stop making love. How easy to simply worship her as if she were a goddess.

Her lips were only a fraction of an inch from his, large and full, shining in the flickering firelight.

Here was a woman he would turn in to the authorities when they got back to civilization—a woman who had killed and lied, who had started this whole trip and been responsible for it from the beginning. She would do anything to have things go her way. She had played two men against each other, for her own purposes. Yet, regardless of this, it was impossible to be blind to her electric powers and her exciting form.

She was the Goddess of Love. Her power was overwhelming.

Then her lips covered his, hungrily. He put his arms around her, almost against his will.

Then she broke away from the embrace and leaned back.

137

"Steve, oh, Steve. We'll be so good together!" she moaned, stretching out her arms toward him. "We're going to be good for one another."

Steve looked at her; a hard lump choked his throat.

So tempting to believe her. So deliciously powerful the drug she had become over his will, mind and imagination.

How could he turn in such a woman?

How was it possible to turn down the offer that she was making?

He'd been a bum for a long time—but a bum who made his own way, his own honest daily living. Could he possibly change, become what Virginia wanted him to become?

Wouldn't that be far easier than putting this beautiful woman behind bars, in a world where no man could touch her?

Oh, God, what a horrid fate; what a waste. Rather keep her on this island. The two of them together. Forever. Better that than all the alternatives he could imagine.

The hardness in his throat lumped tighter and suddenly he looked away, unable to think about what jail would do to such a woman. And, far worse, how could he make love to the woman whom he would turn against? And it would be love. For he loved every delicious inch of her body. No matter what she was.

He stood still. Then turned away.

"Steve...what's wrong?" Virginia cried, alarmed.

"Nothing!" he managed in a choked voice.

"*Something's* wrong!" she snapped.

Steve heard her standing. Suddenly he felt her warm body pressed against his back. Her arms circled under his, around his chest. Her lips found his neck.

"What's wrong, love?" she murmured. "What's wrong? I need you—I need you more than anything in the world."

Steve tried to find the words, but they wouldn't come. He tried to fight down the building desire.

"Virginia, you shouldn't...you don't understand how things are. You shouldn't—do things that..."

"Why not?"

"You have no idea what you do to a man!"

"Oh, yes I do," she murmured in delight. "I know exactly what I do." And her fingers circled down over his chest, lower in a playful tease. "Oh, I know what I do to a man, love!"

"Oh, damned!" he cursed, realizing how quickly he was being sucked into a deep well, from which he could not possibly escape.

It didn't matter what might happen in the following days. Only the moment counted. This delicious heaven was her body.

God he could hardly not love such a woman! The passion welled up through his whole being, as if he'd been shot with a powerful drug. He simply couldn't resist any longer.

Her voice murmured softly.

"You don't have to love me...just take me. I don't care if you don't love me. That doesn't matter," she cried. Her arms tightened around him. "I need you...Steve. I need you more than life itself."

It was almost possible to believe those words. And he just didn't care any more. He turned into her arms and their bodies surged hungrily against one another.

After that it was impossible to think; to consider what he was doing. She was in possession of him completely. He couldn't turn her down, couldn't think about the horror of what would happen when they returned to civilization.

Not until Virginia moved against him did his anguish lessen. There was no escaping it. He covered her lips with his own.

He dived into the fiery pit that opened up between them, fusing their bodies into one continual furnace of passion that bathed every nerve, muscle, thought, every conscious awareness. It was like an endless tumble through eternity.

The firelight flickered lower. The jungle night sounds blended with the soft murmurs of two primitive savages finding ultimate release in each other.

And only then did they, once more, cling together, gasping in the wonderful, joyous aftermath of their love-making only to find it blooming once more like an ever raging fire that had to be consumed in an even wilder landscape of passion, touches, caresses.

They were taking forever in these lush, lovely moments under the stars, aware of nothing other than the mutual, lingering pleasures that surged around them with every touch, every kiss. They worshipped one another as if they had forever to explore, share and exist in this wonderful place in one another's arms.

Now they were true lovers in a way that only soul-mates can become; one unified being. They murmured to the mere joy of being touched. When

140

it all ended neither of them knew, for eternity just folded over all conscious awareness like a loving blanket of soothing, exhaustive rest as they continued to cling together in their endless lover's embrace.

GOLD LUST, BY CHARLES NUETZEL

❋NINETEEN❋

The next morning they awoke early. Steve's body was marked by the scrape of Virginia's fingers, inflicted the night before. He literally shivered at the memory of what they had shared.

As he looked down at her he wondered how any man could possibly deny this lovely creature anything. What they had done to one another had been an endless exploration of a promise of life-long love. They had discovered a total feast, real passionate love, overwhelming, all-consuming emotional physical and sexual need, a savage animal lusting that was totally beyond control.

He wanted to be with her for the rest of his life.

And that was madness. Insanity. But he could not imagine living without her and he was willingly embrace whatever he needed to do to make it possible, no matter what it might cost.

She was a total drug. And he didn't want be cured from his helpless addiction. It was next to impossible to break her spell.

As long as he looked at her, it was not possible to consider anything but submitting to this wonderful beautiful goddess.

He turned away, washing that image from his mind in a desperate attempt to gain sanity.

He gathered up what few supplies were left, and then picked up the Virgin Idol. Virginia was dressed, and came over to him, slipping her arms around his neck, smiling.

"You are wonderful, Steve. It's going to be good, the two of us. Just the two of us, from now on."

He merely nodded and let her kiss him. Then he gently pushed her away.

"What's wrong?" she asked, almost hurt sounding. "Wouldn't you just love a morning snack?"

He didn't dare look at her.

She reached for him, again. "I never had anything like we had last night. I can't believe what you did to me. It was nothing like…any other man!"

Her body surged against him, almost pleading. "I don't want any other man, ever. Just you. Again and again. Nobody ever did what you did last night. God, I just love you!"

How he wished that were true. How he wished so many things. That it was possible to forget what she'd done to Ed and all the other things that had surrounded her every move since meeting her.

He wished it could all wash away from his mind. And wished it was possible to believe her words.

"Later," he managed, huskily. "We can enjoy it all later, again and again. If that's what you want."

"Oh, God, Steve, I don't want anything else but you."

Hope flickered in his imagination. "And the statue? The—"

"Oh yes, that too. We can share all that together somewhere. Travel the world in each other's arms.

Just the two of us, re-experiencing what we had last night."

Could anything be relived? Nothing was the same. Things changed. Moments passed. Time altered reality. Their heavenly ecstasy might very well be the only utter perfection they could ever share.

"We'd better follow this stream to the ocean. It won't be hard to find the plane after that."

"I guess you're right, love," she murmured softly. "I can't wait to do it again...oh we were wonderful together. Oh, so wonderful!"

As they started out, his thoughts returned to what lay ahead of him. And the doubt that had sparked the night before in Virginia's arms now burst into a dangerous flame. It would be so damned simple, so easy, to do exactly what she wanted. And then the world would be theirs, together. Always together—with this guilt, with the pain of knowing the awful price of her love.

They followed the stream until it opened wider. The jungle gradually thinned and they found themselves facing a long stretch of sandy white beach. The ocean waves breaking on the sand had sent their sounds to them for some minutes before they actually came upon the beach.

Both of them stopped on the shoreline, looking at the beautiful sight of the Pacific Ocean breaking against the white sand.

The sun was still high in the sky, baking down upon them.

Everything seemed strangely different. From the hot tropic jungle to the sandy beach, it all seemed miles in distance, worlds apart. It was hard to believe what had happened the day before. This was much like any other beach one would find anywhere in the world. Maybe more beautiful than some, but strikingly familiar.

Virginia turned and smiled. So like a little child, so beautiful and womanly. Her eyes, wide and as blue as the ocean, looked into his, innocently, wonderingly.

"Oh, it would be easy to spend a lifetime here, wouldn't it, Steve?" she murmured, moving closer to him. "It is beautiful, isn't it?"

Steve slowly lowered the heavy weight of the Virgin Idol and dropped it to the sand. His tired muscles relaxed and he let out a long, slow sigh of relief.

Such a lovely dream— the two of them here together for a lifetime.

Virginia looked so appealing, he thought, annoyed by the fact that she did appeal to him in such a powerful way. It was totally impossible not to love her.

Maybe they could make it here, together, away from civilization, the world that had all those horrid rules and high sounding morality. Alone together, here, in this isolated paradise, they could create their own illusion, their own civilization with its own special rules. And nothing else would matter.

"Yes," he managed, gazing at this woman he so loved, who could create such magnificent union with him in such a loving, wonderful way, who was ultra passionate, lusting womanhood without limits.

Who cared?

If only he didn't care.

She sat down on the sand and looked up at him. "Steve, just think. Sandy beaches, expensive hotels, living off the fat of the land. And all for free! All for the taking. You know what these treasures are— public domain, in a way. Good for the taking. Gee, just think. And now it's all mine—ours!" She patted the sand next to her.

Steve sank down, trying to think of something other than the events which must take place when they got to civilization.

They sat there for some time, enjoying the hot sun, the sandy beach, resting after their long hike through the jungle. He kept thinking that the price hadn't been quite as free as she was claiming—and that, regardless of everything, Virginia couldn't be trusted as far as she could be thrown.

Finally they stood.

The sun kept baking down. Virginia took off her blouse as they walked next to one another like two nature children. She kept looking at him, grinning. It was quite obvious that she enjoyed displaying herself, enjoyed the excitement he couldn't keep from his eyes.

The sun dipped and the sandy beach narrowed into a rocky strip, alive with the shimmering spray of breaking waves.

Finally they came to a blind, where the cliff cut down into the water. The jungle edged close on their left.

"Now where?" Virginia asked, pertly grinning. "Looks like it's going to be quite a job, doesn't. Just the two of us trapped here together. What a great dream of a trap. How wonderful it could be. Just you and me...well...we could use a nice hotel room. I always love luxury. Don't you?"

He found it hard to keep from reaching out to

touch her.

Steve shrugged and turned and moved into the jungle, pushing his way through the undergrowth. He smiled grimly to himself. Now Virginia would have no choice but to wear her shirt.

The next hour was an anguish of pushing through thickly matted bushes and around tangled vines and low tree branches interwoven into a tight wall.

At times it seemed they were going around in circles. But every once in a while he would hear the surf and know they weren't too far from the shore.

Finally the jungle started lifting and thinning out. At last they came to an open territory, rocky and bleak. Steve headed toward the edge of the cleared land, where the rocks broke away and fell toward the shore far below. He continued along the edge of the cliff. Then suddenly they came to a turning where the cliff cut away and inland.

It was there that he saw the large cove, and off in the distance, the Mary-Lou, his sea plane.

"Well, not far now!" he announced, pointing.

Virginia gave out with a childish shout of joy and hugged Steve. It was so appealing that it was hard to believe this was the same woman who had killed Ed Blondall, in cold blood. Steve had to hold back a shudder.

He looked into her eyes and knew how hard it would be to even think about turning her in. The mental conflict built, tightened, and then slithered away.

No, don't think, he told himself.

Then another plan suggested itself to him.

How easy it would be just to set Virginia Donovan down on some remote island, and let her make her own way back to the States. He could give her a little money, just enough to keep alive, until she found means to support herself.

It would be far easier than turning her over to the police. And actually, he told himself, there was no real proof that she had actually killed Ed Blondall in cold blood. He didn't know for himself, for sure, what actually had happened.

As he looked at Virginia Donovan, Steve wondered if maybe that was the best plan. Wash his hands of the whole affair, give her a chance, and let whatever god watched over her actions deal out his own justice.

He started to walk along the cliff, which now dipped downwards. He tried to think of nothing, attempted merely to enjoy the beauty of Akiki Island, and not worry about what was to come all too soon.

Finally they reached the sandy beach below and started into the cove. Within twenty minutes Steve came to a stop in front of the life raft which had been tied to a tree, on the beach.

He turned and stared at Virginia, feeling the emotional lump harden again.

Such a beautiful woman. He had known that the moment she possessed him, took control of his physical need, she would control his mind and will.

How much control did she really have? If she turned on the full force of her femininity and aimed it at him, could he resist her? Had he resisted her up to this point?

Sighing, Steve lowered the statue into the raft and then took hold of Virginia's hand as she stepped into the rubber raft. A moment later they were moving toward the sea plane which was docked only a few yards away.

❋TWENTY❋

Steve moved into the pilot's compartment; Virginia sat next to the Idol, her eyes gleaming with excitement.

It was all hers—hers to share with whomever she wished. Steve was the first—he would be her first, in a long list of men. And when she was tired of him, she would find others. Conquest over new lovers was a divine thrill, nothing matched that, unless it was the kind of joy and pleasure the two of them had shared the night before. But nothing lasted. She knew that. They had enjoyed their divine moment—and nothing that followed would reach that wondrous peak.

A thrill waved through her. Yes, it was going to be pretty nice.

Steve opened the door between the two compartments. "Want to come up here?"

Virginia nodded and stepped forward and settled into the co-pilot's seat.

"Well, we're off, Steve," she smiled. "Next stop—riches! And heaven in each other's arms, after a nice bath, a martini, a lush dinner in a lovely hotel. Well, okay, we can wait for all that. I can't hold off much longer to devour you once more like last night. You were so wonderful. I don't what that to ever end! Just the two of us, together for a life-time."

Steve started the engines and let them warm up a bit. Then he took a cigarette from the pack in his shirt pocket. He offered her one and lighted it for her.

Finally the man took control of the plane, centering all his efforts into getting it into the air. In minutes they were racing along over the ocean and then swooping upwards as if lifted by some invisible hand.

Slowly the plane rose, then Steve circled around and flew over the island.

"Well, there it all was, for centuries," Steve announced, turning the plane again and heading northward. "Now it goes into the future."

Virginia sighed, relieved. A lot had happened. But now she was finished with the past, too. Finished with Ed Blondall. She didn't have to worry about the man turning against her, taking all the money for himself. Now it was all hers, to do with as she saw fit.

A feeling of wonderful well-being flushed over her. She turned and studied the man next to her.

What a man this guy was. He wouldn't double-cross her. Steve Floyd wasn't that kind of guy. He was the type of man who would be serious and honest and play things straight. Her kind of guy from this moment on. No more bums, no more cheap pick-ups, no more hell, living in the gutter world, the half-world of mere sensation. She could call the turns now, she could make the rules, and when someone didn't play ball, it would be their neck, not hers. No Ralph Donovans to kick her out. She'd do the kicking from now on, until the day she died.

Virginia sighed, let her hand caressed Steve Floyd's shoulder. "You have good arms—good muscles. You're a good man, Steve. The best!"

Steve didn't move. His eyes were frozen to the world outside the plane. His jaw set.

When they were well out above the ocean, Steve turned and looked at Virginia. His eyes were serious, the muscles in his face hard and rigid.

"I'm turning the Idol over to the authorities," he said abruptly. Every muscle in his neck was rigid, ready for instant action.

His words were like a vicious slap in the face. For a moment Virginia couldn't quite believe him. Then, slowly, as the expression on his face registered, she felt a panic grinding at the pit of her stomach.

"You're kidding me, aren't you?" she cried, trying to laugh, but couldn't.

"No. I'm dead serious!" he announced in an icy voice.

For the first time in her life, Virginia was at a loss for words. She just sat there, staring, not quite able to believe it. It didn't seem possible. Everything had been so smooth, so beautiful up until now.

Then the surprise turned into something else.

Something deadly, which smoldered up through her like acid.

"What are you talking about?" she finally managed.

"You heard me. It will be better that way. If there is any possible claim, then we'll find out. The authorities aren't without a sense of justice. And probably you'll get a reward that will be turned over to you, legally."

'Oh, come on! You know what'll happen! You must be kidding! They'll get their grimy hands on it and then that'll be the end of everything! I'm not turning it over to anybody—except for money!" She was furious.

Steve shook his head. "I don't think there's anything you can do about it."

Virginia slumped against the back of the co-pilot's seat. "Okay. Maybe you're right, Steve. I never looked at it this way before." her chest heaved, then she looked up into his eyes. "I mean it, Steve. You're right. I guess you just gave me a start. There's nothing to worry about. We can go to the authorities and tell them the whole story. I won't cause any trouble. You—you should know me better than that. I love you, Steve. I'll do anything you say—anything at all."

The man hesitated for a moment and then slowly relaxed in his chair.

"I'm sorry, Virginia. I just couldn't take a chance. You looked—violent, for a moment, and I just can't do this the way you wanted. If we kept it...didn't turn it in... It wouldn't be right! But if we did, sure, some collector is sure to come along— fast! Just put the word out. You'd be surprised how fast word gets around. But...that wouldn't be right, and we both know it. With the Idol in the hands of the authorities, nothing can happen, and you'll have a legal claim. And, we do have to report what happened. It's safer that way—all around!"

Virginia's mind was racing madly. The sudden turn had left her dazed, but she'd managed to say the right thing just in time. From his point of view, it all seemed logical. Oh, so logical.

And, in a way, it might be. Only thing was, she didn't dare get herself involved with the authorities.

Once they discovered Ed Blondall's body, learned how he'd been killed, it would be the end of her—life and everything.

Somehow she had to take control.

* * * * * * *

Steve sat there, sweating, holding the controls. He felt a series of conflicting emotions. It seemed to him that Virginia had almost agreed too fast. The only thing was, he hadn't known anything else he could have done, except draw a gun on her. Which was not his idea of a very attractive thing to do.

His sudden statement had blurted out. His mind had been churning from the moment he entered the plane, trying to find some way to explain his plans to Virginia, some way to tell her what he had to do. Then suddenly the words had blasted out, as if some other being was controlling him.

It had been a foolish move. Yet he hadn't been able to resist it. Honesty. Now he felt damned silly, foolish. It hadn't been intelligent. Yet, on the other hand, she seemed to have taken it pretty well, considering.

As he continued on across the Pacific, a feeling of elation surged slowly through him. Maybe Virginia wasn't all as bad as she seemed. Maybe she had, in reality, been merely a girl who was trapped by circumstances, desperate for a stake in life. Maybe she had actually told the truth in the long run.

155

He remembered how she'd been earlier—on the beach. So childlike, so innocent, so wonderful. And the more he thought about it, the more Steve started to doubt his own judgment. After all, the statue had been there on the island for centuries; it belonged to nobody. It was up for grabs. Anybody who found it had a right to do with it as they pleased. Maybe, if things were reported to the authorities, they would believe that she was lying. And what if she hadn't been? What if circumstances were against her?

Steve turned to look at Virginia, and saw the beauty in her face, the childlike perfection of her features. She was a woman. Such beauty was good; how could she be anything other than she appeared? Could evil really exist under that lovely mask?

Yes, it would be so easy to turn his course, to go to another island, make a few contacts, get the Virgin Idol melted down and sell it. Hard cash and a beautiful woman.

He returned his gaze to the control, looked out at the clouds surrounding the plane, down across the blue Pacific. The temptation welled high in him and slowly took control.

Virginia shifted in her seat. Then she unstrapped herself, reached over and touched his shoulder. "I'll be right back. The ladies room calls!"

She laughed casually and then left the compartment.

Steve made up his mind, then. He couldn't take the chance—couldn't endanger this wonderful female.

Checking the compass, Steve dipped the right wing and headed toward an island where he could set down. He would find a hotel where they could stay, then make some contacts with a few men he knew. It wouldn't be that hard.

He was just righting the course when the door behind him opened again and Virginia entered.

Her voice was harsh, cold, demanding. "We aren't going back to the authorities, Steve. We're heading toward Sumatra. I can make arrangements, then. And we'll see what can be done with you. Nobody is going to rob me of that money. It's mine! And I'm not taking any chances—even for you! I'll kill anybody who stands in my way! Ed made that mistake and you just made the biggest mistake in your ever-loving life! You should have had me for a...while, at least. It would have been nice together...for a while."

He felt the cold contact of steel on his forehead.

"Now play it smart, lover boy, and nothing will happen to you! I'd just as soon kill you now, and take my chances in the raft! Understand!"

He felt a chill rush over him. Sick, disgusted, Steve Floyd cursed himself for a damned stupid fool but he couldn't suppress an ironic chuckle

"What's so funny" she snapped in a cruel, cutting voice, sitting in the co-pilot's seat

He turned to look at her "You just blew your chance. I was heading to another place, one where we could have turned the Idol into cash. You had me going. I was feeling sorry for you. I guess you really have a power over me. It fooled me—and I guess it fooled Ed Blondall, too"

Steve pulled the steering wheel back and the plane rose. He continued his course, gaining altitude. There was only one way to turn the tables, but he would need height, and a lot of it. He continued climbing, aware of the deep heavy breathing of the woman beside him.

Then she spoke, almost angrily. "I would have done—anything but what you asked, Steve. If I'd only known!" Her voice was bitter, biting. "What a damned shame! We could have had so much fun together. While it lasted."

Steve looked at her for a moment just before he put the plane into a dive, releasing the controls, letting it go into a slow spin which would pick up speed as they neared the ocean, thousands of feet below.

In the first look he saw a child, crushed, defeated. Then a loud piercing scream sounded from the woman. Her eyes widened and her mouth trembled open as she was thrown against the control panel.

Steve moved fast; there wasn't much time. He had to overpower her, quickly. Had to make it impossible for her to do anything more. Put her out of the running, completely. He leaped from the seat and dived for Virginia. He'd been prepared for the twisting action of the dive, but even then it was almost impossible to control his actions.

The woman was already recovering from her shock. To his amazement, she turned, leveling the gun at his gut, her eyes screaming hate.

"Stop it!" she yelled. "Stop it, now!"

He slammed against the control panel and then was shoved backwards against his seat. Virginia had taken a good hold on the co-pilot's controls and was steadying herself fairly well.

Steve grabbed hold of his controls and then grinned, leaping toward Virginia.

He was gambling that she wouldn't pull the trigger. Or that, if she did, her aim would be off.

His guess was over half wrong.

The barrel exploded flame and he felt a searing heat burn his right side, just as he collided with her.

His hands reached for the gun, grabbed her wrist and then twisted brutally. Then something happened which put out the lights for a split second.

He felt something ram up between his legs; pain blinded him, electrified every muscle. Then the woman was all claws, all writhing cat.

All he could think of was that there couldn't be more than a few seconds left, that time was running out. He was fighting for his life. It didn't matter that this was a woman. She was a threat to his life. She was going to kill them both.

With that, Steve swung. He put all the strength of his right arm into the blow. His fist slammed into something soft and yielding. He heard the woman scream, moan. He struck again, his eyes open, this time aiming the blow at her face. His fist smashed into her jaw, and he didn't wait to find out how much damage he'd done.

Frantically he reached for the controls, pulled himself into the seat, and fought with all his strength to right the plane.

The dive had been long, and the speed had picked up fantastically. The ocean was twisting and turning around and around directly below. Every thought, every nerve went into the struggle. It seemed to take forever. The ocean was racing upwards, faster and faster.

He pulled hard, his body sweating. In that moment, truly facing death, Steve found his mind moving coolly, carefully, as if he were watching a movie in slow motion. There wasn't any real emotional feeling of terror—only a desperate need to do everything in his power to right the plane.

Slowly, but seemingly much too slowly, the nose started leveling out.

The water was rushing faster and faster toward him, like a solid wall.

Then suddenly, much too close for comfort, Steve felt the plane level off, then zoom upward almost into a complete circle. All at once he found himself flying upside down. He thought about Virginia and then turned the plane, righting it. Setting the automatic pilot, Steve stood shakily. He found the woman wedged between the co-pilot's controls and the chair.

For a long time he stood there, breathing hard, sweating, his hands shaking. Then he finally got the strength to move the woman. A few moments later he had her free from the controls and dragged her body out of the compartment.

He found rope, and after lifting her into one of the chairs, he tied her hands and feet, then tied the loose end of the rope to the chair.

Then he returned to the controls.

He corrected the course for home, feeling a deep sense of depression. After that he checked his wound, which was minor, luckily. Where she'd whacked him in the groin had subsided a bit, and would pass. What counted was he lived. All else was a minor matter of healing. The emotional pain, too, would subside. He would survive.

How close he had come. How narrow the line between temptation and sanity. How near he had moved to that shadow land from which he would never have been able to escape.

Virginia Donovan—lovely, seductive, wonderful, child-like, but a hellish bitch. He had found love in hell with a woman who was pure animal on fire, and almost had been sucked to his doom.

It was some time before the depression lifted and another emotion replaced it. In a few hours he would be home, and it wouldn't be like any homecoming he'd ever experienced in his life. After checking with a doctor to make sure he was wounds were patched, he'd would wash the sweat and dirt off his body and soul.

He had also discovered that it was possible to care, to feel, to totally embrace a new woman in his life. Not this one, of course. Just somebody out there in the big world would be waiting for a man to worship her. People were hungry for love; everybody needed to be wanted. It was simply a matter of finding the right person to love. And his heart was once again open to that possibility.

The years of just lounging around, aimlessly, drifting without any purpose, were over. The golden Virgin would be turned over to the proper authorities, and whatever honest percentage was offered as a "finder's fee" would probably be enough to set him up pretty nicely.

The world looked better than it ever had since his wife's death. Her memory would always linger in his life—as would the obsessive nightmare that had been Virginia Donovan. But both experiences were a part of the past that couldn't really hurt him any more.

The world was full of people who simply

wanted to be. Nobody would be exactly like his wife, and hopefully never like this woman in the plane beside him.

The magnificent ancient culture which had designed the Virgin Idol offered the best lesson of all. Life was too short to toss it away. One had to grab it by the guts and live it fully.

Hope, for the first time in years, surged through Steve. The last days had been hellish, but going through them had opened a new window into the future. And he was now flying right through it!

The sun was setting in the west when he gently dipped the plane down toward the ocean and the plane slowly settled down into a foamy landing. He taxied into the little harbor cove, and home.

❁ABOUT THE AUTHOR❁

Charles Nuetzel was born in San Francisco in 1934, and writes:

"As long as I can remember I wanted to be a writer. It was a dream I never thought would materialize. But with the help of Forrest J Ackerman, who became my agent, I managed to finally make it into print.

"I was lucky enough not only in selling my work to publishers but also ending up packaging books for some of them, and finally becoming a 'publisher' much like those who had bought my first novels. From there it as a simple leap to editing not only a sci-fi anthology, but a line of sci-fi books for Powell Sci-Fi back in the 1960s. Throughout these active professional years I had the chance to design some covers and do graphic cover layouts for pocket books & magazines."

Much of his work in covers and graphics are a result of having had a father who was a professional commercial artist, and who did a number of covers for sci-fi magazines in the 1950s and later for pocket books—even for some of Mr. Nuetzel's books.

In retirement he has become involved in swing dancing, a long time lover of Big Band jazz. But more interestingly world travels have taken him (and his wife Brigitte) across the world, to Hawaii, Caribbean, Mexico, Kenya, Egypt, Peru, having a life-long interest in ancient civilizations. His website is full of thousands of pictures taken during these trips.